THE KICKAZZ AFFAIR

It's Fair Game

Shanel WOO

Paperback: ISBN-13: 978-1-7359211-1-2
Ebook: ISBN-13: 978-1-7359211-0-5

Printed in the United States of America

To every woman who has ever been cheated on because they couldn't give their significant other everything they have ever wanted.

Special thanks to my readers for your support.

CHAPTER 1

The Firm

Morning sex was always the best from doggy style, cowgirl, and 69. Sex like that made me want to skip my morning workouts and sometimes my morning coffee depending on how good it was. I would've skipped both, but I loved my coffee. I figured if I kept giving Marshall that good shit, he would continue to keep his thang in his pants for once.

"You okay, babe?" I slipped on my red robe as I sat at the end of our king-sized bed, looking at my physique in our mirror sliding doors.

"Yes, I'm good," Marshall shouted over his shoulder from the bathroom.

"What are you going to do today?"

"Can't do too much after what we just did," he chuckled.

Marshall and I had been struggling in our relationship for years, and I wished our marriage would have gotten better. We had been married for about two years, and I hoped sometime soon that he would have stopped cheating. Everything had been good longer than usual, except that he stayed looking in his damn phone, but I did not pay any attention to that because I had my hands tied with other things.

"I let out a round in you, so maybe today will be the day," he said, striking a pose before smoothing his hand over his mustache and beard with grooming gel. He wore a white terry cloth towel around his waist secured with a twisted knot.

Before I responded, I walked over to our on-suite bathroom where he posed. "We will just have to wait and see." I squirted some gel into the palm of my hand and rubbed more gel into his beard. His diamond-shaped face and high cheekbones hide well under his full dark beard. His beard brought all the attention to those big, soft, pinkish lips. I stood on my tippy toes and gave him a sweet kiss on the lips. I wiped the rest of his grooming gel I had on my hand on his towel. He stood about 6'2". With 6' heels we were almost the same height.

"I am going to have to bust one in you tomorrow, too. Might just start bustin' in you every night from here on out," he laughed.

I wished that were true because lately, our sex life had not been where it needed to be for a couple trying to have a baby.

My cell phone rang and the light blinked and reflected off the slanted 8' by 10" picture of Marshall and me on the nightstand. I grabbed Marshall's watch to see what time it was. "Its nine-thirty, already."

"What's wrong?"

"Oh, Shoot, Its Lori," I shouted.

Marshall looked at me as I ran around and collected different clothing from each side of our master bedroom floor. "Is everything okay?" He raised his slashing eyebrow. He continued to watch me run around like a maniac. "I asked was everything okay?" he laughed

My phone chimed. I had gotten a voicemail. Something told me it wasn't going to be a good one.

I turned on the shower faucet. 'Oh shoot, I am late. I am late." I ignored Marshall subconsciously. I had been late for the last couple of Saturdays meeting with her. I hoped she didn't think I had been acting funny towards her. I was busy with meeting different people to talk about opening my own firm. No one seemed to fit my standards.

Lori and I are cousins and we're born one day apart. She and I meet every Saturday morning to talk about girl things. Girl's things usually end up being gossip between our workplaces. Like the previous week, so many things happened, from one of my co-workers urinating in my other co-workers lemonade he left in our office's fridge. They dated, and he broke it off with her because she became too obsessed with him. She became a straight looney toon, but she had always been a little off to me.

They finally found out who was my bosses' secret admirer. She would write him letters and send them to the office. Plue, she would spray the letters with a potion she called her Pussy Juice. She took his small words of encouragement as a sign that he wanted to fuck her. She was having a hard time with her relationship, and he told her she deserved better in dealing with men, and she took it and ran with it. Oh yeah, I still hadn't told Lori that I saw one of my co-workers on TV. He talked to this girl for about two years, and she turned out to be a he. So embarrassing. Cool Jay was not so cool anymore around the office. Cool Jay was someone who would always flirt with Lori when she came to see me at the office.

My phone rang again. I ran over to the nightstand and snatched it up. It tumbled on my fingertips, but I caught it before it fell onto the floor. Lori's name lit up in the display, and underneath her name, it read two missed voice-mails. I checked the voicemails before jumping in the shower. The level of anger in her voice decided if I would take a relaxing shower or a hoe sink bath. I walked into the bathroom and grabbed my shower cap from the side of the sink.

"You have two new voicemails...message one."

Lori yelled, "Bitch, I know you see me callin' you. Why the fuck is you still at home? That's okay. I'm about to bounce bihhh!"

"Lori is funny," Marshall laughed and tapped the razor blade on the edge of the sink. He put it back up to his beard and continued to line himself up.

"Yes, you know its Lori."

He shook his head in agreement.

Lori and I had a cousinship. We were so close to one another. We had to be because if anyone ever tried to call me a bitch, the results wouldn't be pleasant.

"Message two."

Lori yelled again, "Biiihhhhhhh!"

"End of messages."

She rarely got any time off, but when she did, she wanted to spend it with me. She worked at one of the most popular/busiest marketing agencies in the city, and she was very good at what she did. With all the wild ass crazy things she did in college, she still graduated Magna Cum Laude. She got her degree in business marketing, and she graduated with Marshall's sister, Maxine.

"Ouuchhh," I screamed. The water hit the crease of my back and was hot as hell.

"Are you okay in there?" Marshall turned to look toward the shower where I was standing.

From the voicemails, Lori left. I needed to make that

shower a hoe bath. Semen streamed down my leg, and I knew I was going to have to say sorry to Lori because I needed to wash my entire ass before I went anywhere.

"Yes, I'm good. Just wasn't ready for the water to be this damn hot," I answered, not to unintentionally ignore Marshall again.

"Relax," he suggested. He put down his razor and walked out of the bathroom.

After 15 minutes of cleansing the sex away, I brushed my teeth and sprayed my pulse points with my favorite perfume. It smelled of vanilla and flowers. I started calling it my own personal 'Pussy Potion' perfume.

I grabbed my black romper from my walk-in closet, but that day I felt sexier than usual, so I grabbed my red romper instead. I matched my romper with a pair of my favorite red bottoms.

"I am going downstairs,' Marshall said to me as he stared in his phone with a smile. I ignored how distracted he was with his phone because he looked so good in his gray jogging pants and black short-sleeved v neck shirt. The watch I got him for our first anniversary looked decent with whatever he put on.

"Do you think you could make me a pot of coffee while you are down there?" I laid my romper across my naked body, shifting my shoulders front to back while looking in my mirror sliding doors.

"Yes, I can. You can have whatever you liiike." His smile shifted from his phone toward me. "I don't need any after what we just did this morning, but I'll toast to that good, good," he laughed.

"Right!" I agreed. Marshall was funny and rarely got mad about anything. Well, he hadn't got stupid in a long time.

Marshall walked out of the room, and I started to vogue. "Damn, I look good," I complimented myself as I spun around in a full circle. I could never go around Lori looking a mess. She thought I was her personal super-model, and I don't know how when I dragged all that ass. I think that's why Marshall loved me so much. He was either with me because I had a nice round shaped ass, or because he knew I was a dumbass and wouldn't leave.

I pulled my hair from my shower cap. Thank God my beautician slayed my hair because my natural big curly hair would not have survived that humid, hot shower. I made the bed before heading to the kitchen to grab the rest of my things. I was always the one who fixed the bed. Marshall could never make the bed how I liked it. I couldn't remember the last time he even attempted to try.

I looked down at my phone. Lori had called about forty-five minutes before I walked out the door. It only took thirty minutes for me to make it to the coffee shop from my house. I snatched both my car keys and coffee cup off the kitchen counter and darted to my car. I grabbed the mail from the mailbox propped up on the side of my driveway and hopped in my shiny emerald green BMW convertible. No one in this neighborhood owned a BMW, and I had never seen a BMW emerald green. I called her My Boss, Money, and Woman Whip.

The birds were chirping, and the sun was smiling. It was a beautiful day. Something good had to happen.

After I quickly browsed through the pile of mail noting I had credit card limit increases, I slid them in my glove compartment. I pulled my visor down to look in the mirror, making sure I had the appropriate coverage on my lips and breast. Last time I rushed out of the house,

I had red makeup smeared across my lips. So, after that time, I made sure I didn't look like the joker stepping out again.

My neighborhood was one of the best villages to reside in. My neighbors walked their löwchen dogs like clock-work, and a few of my neighbors would jog along the side of the streets with their expensive headphones propped on their ears. The blocks were long and full of beauti-ful homes and beautiful well-manicured lawns. "Best on Earth" by Russ ft. Bia played on my stereo. I turned it up on full blast. My bougie neighborhood didn't stop my ra-chet from jumping out.

The security guard greeted me at the gate. But before I pulled up, I turned my radio down a couple of notches.

"Hey, Mrs. Valentine. I haven't seen you in a while. You usually just scan your key pass to exit the gate." He walked over a couple of inches to my car. He wiped the crumbs from the corners of his mouth that showed that he'd been secretly eating.

"Hi, Hayes. I stopped because you were approaching the window. Half the time, I don't know it's you. But so nice of you to come out and say hi." Hayes had always been eye candy. He wore an all-black uniform. It fit him perfectly and showed off his aggressively built frame. He was well-shaven and smelled so sweet.

"Are you off to enjoy the weather? It's as beautiful as you this morning." His eyes focused on my breast then up to my face. "Your eyes are green today? Does that mean Something special is going to happen?"

My eyes changed colors, depending on how I felt. "Yes, I am off to enjoy this beautiful day, and I hope something special does happen, but how have you been?"

"I've been doing great. Although my girlfriend and I

just broke up." He faked a cry and then shook his head while his chin touched his chest. Before he looked back up, he wiped his fake tears with the sides of his hands. "Long story, but I've been...yeah... I've been great." He smiled with his surprisingly cute crooked smile. "I wish I could be out enjoying the weather in the city. I get off in a couple of hours. I'll be heading out soon, though."

"Oh, okay, cool. That's good to hear. Have fun!" Hayes probably had at least five girls. His glooming brown eyes were most definitely a trap. From the way he always looked at me probably wanted me to be the sixth girl he kept in his little black book .

"Thanks, Mrs. Valentine. You enjoy yourself out there." He buzzed me out.

Lori stared at me from the patio. Her teeth clenched, and her fingers were tapping the glass table so aggressively. She frowned upon my arrival. I found her face so funny. I couldn't laugh, though, because she would've flipped out. I came up with all kinds of lies on the way to our table.

Hey girl, my car broke down.

Hey girl, I had to stop at the gas station. Can you believe I ran out of gas?

When did the gas prices go up?

Girrrrl, let me tell you. I got a flat tire.

But she wouldn't believe any of that. Shit, I wouldn't even believe that shit myself.

"I am so sorry. Traffic was a mess." I approached our table.

Lori's right leg overlapped the left. Her thighs gripped to each other. She had on her new hot pink midi dress that she bought the week before. She talked about me being a supermodel, and she was just like me. We never wore the same thing twice. Her size 34 double D cup breast hugged together and sat on the top of the dress, which laid on the black table.

I pulled my chair from the table and propped my backside down in it. Lori cocked her head to the right. "Bish, you are lying. I tracked your phone when I got here, and you were still at home," she said with a whole attitude. She straightened her head. "You better be lucky I ran into an old friend, or I would've left. As a matter of fact, I think you can benefit from our conversation. The guy I ran into name is Cole. He works for the top investment company, and he specializes in three areas: public relations, marketing, and investments. Maybe he can help you start up your firm," she suggested.

"Ain't God good. If I weren't late, you would have never had the opportunity to make my dreams come true." I was being sarcastic. Sometimes that broke the ice between us or made her madder. I forgot which one.

"Yeah, aight bish. But anyway, take down Cole's number, and I'll text him to let him know you will give him a call."

We ordered some coffee. I know I shouldn't have had any more coffee because I would always get the runs whenever I would drink a lot of it. But I couldn't let Lori know that I had already had a mug or two. She was already mad about me being late.

I got my usual iced coffee with extra milk. But I didn't have to tell the waitress my order because Lori and I were regulars. We had been going to that shop for a long time.

"Girl, I still think about when Marshall and I first met, and he invited me to have coffee with him. I laughed at his ass, coffee? You better take me out to eat! You know girls love to eat. Ha. Ha. Ha"

"Yes, girl, I remember the star quarterback tried to get some ass out of you for the low, low," she burst out laughing and almost ripped her dress down the middle.

"But shit, I needed a lot of coffee to get through those rough days in college. When I had to stay up all night writing papers, those coffees kept me up. Especially on those hot days, those iced coffees would send chills through my body. The same chills Marshall sends through me now." I pondered.

"Yeah...yeah...yeah. I don't think I volunteered to hear all of that nonsense. Never understood wh—"

"Anyways, bish, why did you get the patio table? It's hot as hell out here." I interrupted her rant.

Lori swung her head side to the side with a jerk in her neck. "When a bish can be on time, she can pick the seats, ya feel me?" She rolled her eyes, hard. So hard that I thought they would pop out.

"We had so much fun at that yacht party last weekend. It was turnt up. How'd you find that party?" Lori always knew how to find the turnt up parties, and I never turnt them down.

"It was posted on our alma mater school website." Lori did the prep dance in her seat. Bouncing both hands from side to side.

"I think that's where Maxine got the information about the yacht party we are going to today. You know I am going to meet Maxine at that same yacht party, right?"

She stopped dancing instantly. "Oh, you goin' with that bitch, huh?" she asked, sounding annoyed.

Although Lori and Maxine graduated the same class

year and with the same degree, she still never really liked Maxine. We would always agree; Maxine may be my friend but will always be Marshall's sister. She would have his back before mines, which I understood.

"Yes, I would've invited you, but you don't fuck with her." Lori already knew why she didn't get an invite. She just wanted an invite. It was kinda like her verification that I wouldn't ever put Maxine before her.

"She okay. I don't fuck with her like that, but I love a good party. She don't stop my fun." She rolled her eyes and took a sip of her coffee.

"Plus, you said you had to do some things in the office today." I reminded her.

"You're right." Imitating a game show host. "Contestant number five come on down looking ass," she snickered. "Don't try to make excuses and shit for why you didn't think to invite me."

"I am sorry, girl, damn." I leaned across the table to hug her. She pushed me away. "But anyway, you know Marshall and I have been trying to get pregnant for over a year and a half now, and …it's just not happening." I shook my head and looked down at the table, waiting to hear some kind words from Lori.

"Shit, it's probably because of that abortion and all those damn plan b's you were taking. Bish you were taking them bitches like multivitamins," she cackled while impersonating me taking a pill and gulped it down with the water the waitress brought to our table.

"Bish, I know you are not talking. You were taking them too," I asserted.

"Yeah, I took them because I wanted to. Not because I was forced." Lori took another sip of coffee and side eyed me like she was stating facts.

"Bitch, at least I wasn't dancing on top of tables, and chugging down beers at damn near every party I went to." I had to remind her that she wasn't an angel. "Oh, and let us not forget running through the school with no top on. Boobs just out there and everywhere."

"Girl didn't nobody ask you all of that," she said, upset. She sat there quietly. I could tell she was thinking about it.

"Wait, don't get mad now. You remember when you found out James cheated, and you busted the windows out of his car and flattened his tires."

"I bust the windows outcha car," she harmonized and did the prep dance again.

"Yeah, so don't try to make me feel bad. By the way, how James doin' anyway? Heh heh. Ya'll still together, right?"

"Bitch, you know we are still together, kinda," she said while rolling her almond-shaped eyes.

I started to feel a little bad, but happiness over-powered that because Marshall ain't have shit to give. I mean nothing, but a hard dick and a sexy face.

"Remember, he would break up with you every three months. Remember this, 'I don't want to cheat on you. You know the girls keep callin me,'" she mimicked Marshall. He killed me with that. He had at least two girls, plus you."

"Yeah, I know, right. I was in love with him, and I still am. He was my first real relationship. I think. I didn't have time to get to know anyone else. You know I had a lot of short kiddie relationships. Guys were trying to get at me every day."

"Yeah, like Brian," she inserted.

"But, I still wanted Marshall." I started off to fantasize

about our college days.

"Speaking of Brian. I saw him the other day. Girl, he is fine, fine. He asked about you. I think you should give him a call."

"Bitch, I'm marri—."

"So..." She shrugged her shoulders. "Wait." She grabbed my wrist that laid on the table and laughed out loud. "Ron, does Marshall still think he's your first? Bish, you funny for that shit. Telling that man that lie." A burst of spit flew from her mouth as she laughed harder. Lori's ass always thought I was a comedian.

"Yes." I shouted, "Fuck you! He doesn't need to know that shit."

Marshall thought he took my virginity. The only reason there was blood is because I was coming on my period. I thought about telling him, but I didn't want to hurt his ego.

"But, no for real, Ronnie. I hope everything works itself out with you trying to get pregnant. I am always here for you and whenever you need to talk." She shouted, "But bish, next time, be on time!"

"Okaaayyy." I agreed and pouted.

"I love you so much, girl."

"I love you too." My pout turned into a bright smile.

"Anyway, the bill is on you this time, late ass. I have to go," she said.

"But I thought it was on you this time, favorite cousin." I reached for her purse.

She quickly snatched her purse from the table before I could place a finger on it. "You good. Oh yeah, you have to pay for Cole's coffee too. He wanted to pay, but I told him I would pay.

"Wow... that's how you do me?"

"Yup, I knew that you were going to have to pay for everything with your late ass. Tootles." She shouted, "BYE." She walked to me, kissed me on the cheek, and strolled toward the door.

"But we forgot to talk about our work week," I yelled trying to get her attention so she would turn back around, but she was gone out the door.

"Waitress," I shouted.

Hurry up so I can get the hell out of here and go home. I need to take a damn nap.

My phone vibrated in the front pocket of my purse. Sam lit up in the display.

Are you here yet?

I stared at the text for a second before I realized I was supposed to meet him at the same coffee shop I was sitting in at that very moment. I looked around, and I didn't see him.

Nope, I am sorry. I thought I texted you about rescheduling. I must have forgotten. I lied. *Get a frappe on me.*

Although I haven't met the right counterpart, Sam was the closest match to at least get the ball rolling. But after Lori referred Cole, I decided to see what he was about before signing a contract. That was the last time I would send Sam off. That was not the type of person I was, but lately, I hadn't been in my right mind, and I was fatigued.

While I drove down the shore, I reached in my purse and grabbed my phone. I began to text Cole about his availability to meet up and discuss my firm, and some idiot cut me off. I guess that's why they say don't text and drive. I switched lanes and sped in front of him and got caught by a red light.

He pulled up on the side of me in a black infinity truck. I saw him in the corner of my eye staring at me. Please don't say anything to me, and please don't be an off-duty cop. I didn't want to get in trouble with the law. I checked both side mirrors attempting to look like a safe driver. He turned down his music.

"Hey... hey beautiful," he yelled hesitantly out the window. I acted as if I didn't hear him and slid my bang behind my ear. I turned my head toward the passenger side window.

He drove his car over the crosswalk line. At that very moment, I regretted having 20/20 vision because he was clearly in my peripheral.

"Hey, hey beautiful," he yelled, again, but forcefully. He blasted his music and quickly turned it down. His tactic didn't work.

I continued to ignore him. I turned my music up and did the snake dance.

Beeeeeeep.

I got a huge shock when he laid on the horn. "Damn, can I help you?" My attitude was on a hunnit.

He waved, and his dimpled smile filled his face.

"Yo, strong ass better workout less and drive more." His veins pushed through his arms. His muscular biceps were tight and exceptionally large.

"I'm sorry, but you look great," he complimented.

"You don't scare people like that. You don't know if I had a medical condition or nothing," I ranted. I'll admit. I sounded crazy.

"I understand, and I am sincerely sorry, but I just wanted to tell you that you are beautiful.

"Tell me something I didn't already know... Oh, and next time, make sure you watch what you are doing. You could've caused an accident."

"Ha-Ha, maybe you shouldn't text and drive." He

smiled with a flawlessly healthy smile.

"Damn, what are you a private investigator? I musta really caught your eye."

He held his phone in his hand. "Maybe I am, but before the light changes can I get your num—"

"Whatever, BYE." The light changed just in time. I floored the accelerator.

He was most definitely attractive, but I am happily married.

I glared at my rearview mirror, and he was trailing me. Thirsty much.

He beeped twice before he made a left turn at the traffic light. As if he ever had a chance.

I drove past Gale's house, our next-door neighbor. From the corner of my eye, I could see her in her front yard watering her grass. She drowned her lawn at the very least 30 times a week. I didn't know if she did that to be nosey, or she really wanted to keep her yard manicured.

She always wanted to hang out, but she was not in my age group, and the way Lori was set up, Gale wouldn't have stood a chance with us.

"Hey Ronnie," she shouted across the yard, waving her arm from one side to the other.

Sometimes she can be a little annoying, and if she got my attention, she would talk me to death.

"Hey, Girl. On the phone. Talk to you later." I mouthed and pointed at my phone that I quickly placed to my ear. I didn't care if she knew that I lied or not. "I'll come by later," I shouted across the yard. I lied again.

"Okay, Girl. Don't forget. It's important," she sounded eager.

"Okay." I slammed the door and fell back against it.

Thank God I made it home and managed to get away from that maniac on the road and let's go out, Gale.

"Make it last forever" by Keith Sweat played from the speaker in the kitchen. Marshall stood over the stove as I walked to the far side of our home. The muscles in his back protruded. At the same time, the back of his body-building tank top that he wore although he was never a bodybuilder sat in the middle of his shoulder blades. I stood behind him, and it reminded me of how I stood behind him in the crowd before his football games started. He was smaller than he was when he played back then. Still tall and handsome, though. I walked past without greeting him.

"Hey, Babe." He grabbed my hand and spun me around. He smiled with that gorgeous smile that I always loved. That alluring smile always made my panties wet, but not at that moment. A girl was tired, and I still had not told him I missed my period. I had a doctor's appointment coming up, so I hoped to get some good news. I was tired of false results, but if I were finally pregnant, that would be his surprise graduation present. He slapped my ass after spinning me around and grabbed my wrist to pull me back to him.

"Someone's happy." I smiled, overtired. "You are home early today. Did you leave the house this morning?

"Yes, I went to class, and the teacher canceled last minute. So, I just came back home and finished up on some work. I just walked through the door about five minutes before you walked in."

"Okay. Well, I am going to lay down. I've had a long morning. See you in a bit." I grabbed Marshall's dick, pulled him down to my level, and kissed him on the lips. He jumped with excitement. I loved teasing him, so when it was time, it was time.

When I got to the room, a sour smell reached every square inch. I sprayed the air fresher that sat on the bathroom sink. I sprayed as I searched for the source. Too tired to finish, I tossed the freshener and my phone on our unmade bed. I jumped headfirst into my pillow. I had been waiting to get back to bed since I woke up that morning and nothing else was going to stop me. I set my alarm.

Buzz. Buzz. Buzz.

My back raised off the bed as I lifted into a sitting position. I was well rejuvenated. It was time to go and party. I reached over and turned the alarm off, and our picture laid flat on its face. I sat it back up.

Marshall walked into the bedroom, sat on the bed behind me, wrapped his arms around me, and kissed me on the side of my neck. "How are you feeling?"

"I am feelin' fine." I walked over to the closet and grabbed my jumpsuit from its hanger. That jumpsuit was never my first pick. I never really liked it too much. It fitted too big. The bottom of the pants legs would get stuck under the heels of my shoes. I finished pulling my legs through the pant's legs. "How do I look?" I asked.

"You look good." His eyes focused on his phone.

"You ain't even looking, loser." I snapped my fingers at him for his attention.

He looked up and smiled, blowing a kiss right after. "I said you look good baby."

I walked over to the mirror, taking a good look at myself. "Shiiit, I know I do." Marshall had been clingy lately. Always in my space. I didn't mind though I loved his company; it was just an awkward feeling. Maybe he was just super excited about his graduation, and I gave him positive vibes. Even so, he was always on that damn phone.

"What's going on in that phone?" I placed my hand on my hip and my rotated my head in a circle. "I am getting tired of seeing you smile at this point."

"Nothing, baby. Just looking at stuff about my graduation. "He stood up and walked closer to me.

Shit, I graduated too, and I wasn't on my phone that damn hard. That man acted like he is was going to be the first man to walk on the moon.

"I let you enjoy your graduation, didn't I?" he continued.

"Barely, you were out there cheating, REMEMBER, but we are not going to talk about that. We are in a different space. I am going to finish getting dressed so I can go meet up with your sister."

"Okay, I hope you two have fun." He scrolled through his phone some more.

"Me too." I put my hands on my knees and shook my ass. I tried to shift Marshall's attention from his phone to me.

"Haha. Stop playin' with me." Marshall ran over to me and wrapped his arms around me. "Stop playin' with me," he whispered in my ear.

Shaking my ass worked.

"Make sure Maxine doesn't get too drunk." He unwrapped his arms from around me and took a couple of steps back, looked me up and down checked me out.

"You better hope I don't get too drunk," I mumbled.

"What did you say?" He tackled me in the bed and kissed me all over my face. "Better stop playin' with me."

"Hahaha. I didn't say, anything baby." I struggled to get him off me.

He finally let me go, and I walked to the bathroom.

He could be so admiring. That was precisely why I fell in love with him in the first place. He watched me from a distance with those big brown eyes. He walked toward the door.

"I'll be downstairs if you need me." He grabbed his dick through his shorts and jerked it toward me.

"I'll be down after I do my makeup." I pushed my tongue in and out of my cheek. I gave him the illusion of me sucking his dick.

I looked for my comfortable white heels. I remembered that I left them in Marshall's car. I grabbed the spare key and headed to his car. When I walked through the kitchen to the sliding door, Marshall stood on the opposite side of the kitchen island, smiling and grinning at his phone. When he saw me, he laid his phone on the kitchen island.

"Hmm, what are you smiling about baby." I acted interested.

"Nothing, just on the school's site looking at the graduation stuff. Just excited, that's all."

I walked over to his side of the island and picked his phone up. Graysville University in big, bold letters of his school's website jumped out at me.

"You thought I was lying," he laughed and grabbed his phone from my hand. A text came through, but I couldn't read the name.

"No, I don't. I am just so happy for you, baby, and I can't wait. I'll see you in a bit."

"Okay, Baby, have a great time," he said as I closed the sliding doors.

I checked the inside of his car on the backseat and floor. My shoes were not there. They were not in the trunk either, but a dress that didn't belong to me laid across his gym bag. It was a midi size blue dress. I remembered that Maxine borrowed his car the other day while hers was in the shop. I locked up and jumped in my car, rolled my windows down, and blasted my music, backing out the driveway. I wanted to enjoy my rachet music without being bothered by Gale.

I pulled up to a stop sign. "Ghetto booty, pretty face, thick thighs," I sang loud and clear. A heavyweight short man with jogging pants and a striped shirt stared at me while walking his dog. I let them walk across because he stopped dead cold in front of my car. He stared me dead in my face. I mean, he didn't focus on anything else. Maybe he stopped because my music was loud. I honked my horn to let him know a car was speeding directly toward him, almost hitting them.

"Get out of the god damn street," the driver yelled out of the window.

"Man, fuck you," he yelled back. "Thanks, beautiful," he shouted to me.

I dun saved his staring ass life. By the time I made it to the highway, traffic was a mess. A girl was hanging out of the passenger side window while the driver sped. I sat and stared at them for a couple of seconds before reaching to turn my music down. I didn't want people to think that we were all together.

After being stuck in traffic for 20 minutes, I finally pulled up to the yacht party. Valet came over to grab my keys. He looked like he had a couple to drink. He had tip money hanging from his pocket. If it had fallen out of his pocket, it was going to be mine. I would've given it back to him, though. I would've just acted like it was my tip to him.

"Don't put a scratch on it!" My keys hung from my

index finger off in front of me at eye level.

The valet driver grabbed them. "I'll be sure not to ma'am." He walked off. I didn't trust him to drive, but he would pay if he damaged my baby. Believe me.

"Can you stop the elevator, please?" A tall, slender man ran full speed toward me. My finger pressed against the closing door button didn't stop him from making it through the doors.

"Can you press five?" he asked.

Why couldn't you press five? You have the same numbers on your side of the elevator.

"Five?... Sure." He wore a polo shirt and fitted jeans. His feet looked extremely comfortable in his size eleven or twelve sized loafers. He smelled expensive.

"I am not from around here," he explained.

I never knew why people thought I liked talking to them. "Oh, you're not? Where are you from?" I waited silently for a ding from the elevator and stared at the floor indicator. I prayed that floor three would approach quickly. I did not want to chat with him any longer. Not even for a second.

"I am from the mid-west." He smiled. He extended his hand for a handshake.

I've never heard anyone describe where they were from by the region. Maybe I should've been impressed, but I wasn't. "Oh, really. I bet it's nothing like how it is here." I lifted my hand to that side of my face with a slight smile rejecting his polite handshake.

"Actually, I like..." he lowered his hand and straightened his shirt. "I like it here. It's a lot of pretty women here, such as yourself."

He didn't get the message. "I'm flattered." I lied.

"True." We both stared at the floor indicator.

Level three approached a second after. "Okay, well, I hope you have a nice time here." I sashayed off the elevator.

"Okay, thanks, beautiful," he shouted.

To my surprise, I got off the elevator, and Maxine stood a couple of feet away with a drink propped in her hand. Maxine was sluggin'. Her booty was FAT. Maxine had always been the girl who thought she could pull any man who came her way and then turned around and says she doesn't need a man when it doesn't work out. She was cute, had an attractive frame, and with a little makeup, she probably could pull a few more men.

"It's about time you got here. You have been late a lot lately," she complained.

"Well, your brother and I were." I put both my hands in a palming ass position and motioned the doggy style move.

"That was something you could've kept to yourself," she said. Her face frowned up.

"Welp, I thought you should know. Ha ha haaa."

"Girl, not really," she replied with her dropped chin.

"Where are you sitting?"

"Outside on the patio. Over there." Maxine pointed in the direction of our seats.

"Ayeeee, Yes, sounds like a plan to me." Maxine always spoiled me. The patio area was VIP. Just like me V I-Muh-tha-fuckin' P.

"I thought you would agree." she smiled and then laughed.

On our way to our section, I stopped by the bar. The bar was packed like a can of Vienna sausages. People were standing so close on each other you would've thought we were at an orgy party. To make matters worse, there were only two bartenders and they were moving slower than molasses. I knew right there that we weren't going to be heading to our section any faster than what I imagined.

"Excuse me," I yelled across the crowd for service. I stepped on the footstep and leaned over the bar. "Excuse me." The bartender walked toward me.

"How can I help you?" She said while stuffing money in her bra.

"I want to try something sweet." I couldn't think of anything sweet. I would've just got some champagne, but I wanted to try something new.

"Something sweet? I mean, that could be anything." She looked in the sky like a drink menu was going to appear. She probably just got the job that morning. I wouldn't have been surprised from the way she spoke.

"How can I help you?" The tall thin man who was standing next to her interrupted.

"I was looking to get like a... sweet fruity drink." He looked like a better-educated bartender than she was.

"Okay, I got you. I have just the drink." The bartender was wreathed in smiles. His smile fell off to the side. Rather flirtatious.

"Thank you." I smiled politely.

"No, thank you!" He winked. He stood in front of me and made the drinks.

"You know what, can you make that two fruity drinks?" I didn't want to have go back to the bar and deal with the crowd or ole girl.

I walked back over to where Maxine was standing.

"I noticed that your hands are both full. You are trying to get messed up, huh?" she giggled.

"Sure am. But no, I just didn't want to have to go back and wait."

"Good thinking. I should've done the same."

As we made our way to our patio sitting, the DJ called out for all the women to twerk. "Watch me while I twerk" by MarQuis Trill placed throughout three SOUNDBOKS speakers. Women started to hop on the couches with their big ass booties shaking from here and there, and I damn near got knocked down by a big short body shaped chick. I had a lot on my mind when I saw Maxine. I couldn't jump into rachet mode and start twerking, not at that moment. We made it to our seats through the large, packed crowd.

"So, you know, Marshall, and I have been trying to get pregnant for a while now, right?" I jumped right into the conversation before we could even sit our full asses in our seats.

"Yes," she said gleefully. "OMG, are you pregnant?" she asked.

"No, that's the problem. I am 32 years old. It's going to be too late. We have been trying and trying nothing seems to be working."

"Have you tried to go see a doctor about it." She crossed her legs. She showed off some thigh through the slit in her dress.

"Yes, they want to run some test on us, but Marshall doesn't want to do it. He says he knows it's not him, and he doesn't need to get checked out."

"Well, that's unfortunate. Marshall needs to check himself too." She stared off over my shoulder and pulled on her skirt to show a little more leg.

"Yes, so if he doesn't go. I am not going. We will just keep trying and hope for the best." I noticed she was still staring over my shoulder, not giving me any eye contact, so I turned around and noticed she was staring at a guy, and he was staring back. "Best on Earth" by Russ ft. Bia started to play.

"Enough with the small talk Max. This is my song. Let's dance." I danced my way back to the bar. I got two more drinks. This time it was grey goose and cranberry. On my way back to my seat, I see the guy who shared an elevator with me. His mid-west ass probably got lost.

"Girl, this party is lit," I yelled to Maxine. At that point, I was too lit. I was twerking on slow songs and stepping on fast. My heel got caught in my pants leg, and I tripped, and my armed bumped into some girl's arm. The bump made both our drinks spill on us. "OMG, I am so sorry," we said in unison. She was medium height, brown skin, thick, with a bone-straight bob.

She grabbed a napkin from the table. She was unbalanced and stumbled. "It's okay. Its clear liquor," she said. "Thank God," we said in unison again.

"Do you need some more napkins?" I asked.

"No, I have more. I see you're turnt up tho," she said, two-stepping. "Yassss, turn up." She was drunk too. Thank God because I am surely not in the state of mind to be fighting. You know how chicks get wanna act all big and bad, but she took it smooth. She and I danced together. The expensive smelling guy from the elevator came over and hugged her.

Oh, so this was her boyfriend—cheating dog ass.

She turned to me. "Hey, this is my little bro--"

He interrupted, "She means her brother. Just brother."

"Hahaha. It doesn't matter. I am married." Even if I wasn't, he wouldn't stand a chance.

"Happily?" he asked.

"Yes, Happily. Thank you." I turned toward Maxine. "By the way, this is my husband's sister, Maxine." I introduced him.

"Hey, how are you?" he said in an uninterested tone. Maxine continued to dance without saying hi back to him. I guess she caught on to his careless demeanor. "Welp, have a great night then." He walked off in the direction of a group of girls.

"Men are so thirsty. I'm so glad we bumped into each other," she said, still dancing.

"Literally, bumped into each other," we giggled.

"I am happily in a relationship myself. So now we can turn these losers down together. By the way, my name is Casey Cox." She introduced herself, pleasantly.

"I know, right. We need a sign that says, 'NO MEN ALLOWED,' right?" we laughed. "My name is Ronnie Lawson." I never used my married name when meeting strangers. It was probably because my husband cheated so much that I didn't want to run into or introduce myself to any of his side chicks.

She and I started to dance together, and Maxine's face was priceless. She motioned with her lips. "Bish, what are you doing?" My friends knew I didn't like people that much, so they are surprised when I mingled. Casey and I partied for a few, and then she and her brother left.

I shouted, "Turn up... It's lit." Those were my favorite words when I was drunk and happy. When I say those words, I'm most definitely having a great time.

"Maxine," I yelled. "Maxine," I repeated. She was busy eyeing that guy from across the way.

When she finished, she walked over to me.

"I forgot to mention that I love your dress. I think you left a dress just like it in Marshall's car."

"A dress like *this*...no it can't be this is the only dress that I ha—"

One of Maxine's best friends walked up and interrupted us and gave her an extremely long hug. She was
dark-skinned, skinny, with long black hair. She tried to
yell over the music to Maxine, "Heyyy girl." In the middle
of the hug, she side-eyed me. "Are you Marshall's wife?"

That bitch knew damn well I was Marshall's wife.
Bitch, we all went to school together. Bitch, you were
trying to talk to him. Thinking you had a better chance
than me because you were his sister's best friend. But you
know what, I kept it cool and classy, although this cranberry and goose was about to get these hands loose on
her ass. I side-eyed her and kept dancing.

"Why is she always so rude?" I heard her say clear as day
when the music stopped to change songs. I chugged down
my drink, dipped to the floor, and rolled my hips slowly
back up to the standing position.

I sobered up a little by the time I left. I walked over
to the valet booth. "Tell me something good, Mr.," I instructed.

"Ma'am?" he said with a wrinkle in his nose and crease
between his eyebrows. He scratched the middle of his
head.

"Tell me something good. Did you or did you not damage my car?"

"Ma'am, I don't know what kind of car you have," he
said and threw his hands up.

I can't believe he acted like I didn't threaten his life
when I gave him my keys. I shouted, "DID YOU OR DID
YOU NOT DAMAGE MY CAR?" The guy who took my keys
tapped my shoulder.

"Ma'am, I think you meant to talk to me, and no, I
didn't damage your car." He smiled compassionately.

"You better not." My eyes were blurry, and I couldn't

see a damn thing. I grabbed my keys. "Thanks, guys." I walked to my car semi stumbling.

I pulled up to the front of my house. I sat in the car and decided to text Cole.

Hey Cole. My name is Ronnie. Lori gave me you r numer. She said you could help me with starting my firm? Please let mee know when you r available.

I opened, closed, squirted, and blinked my eyes for a better view of my text. I fucked up a couple of words, but he knew what I was trying to say.

Yes, I remember. I am available in the morning. We can meet at the coffee shop where I saw Lori today. Is that okay with you? At around nine o'clock a.m?

Yes, that's fine. See you there. I hoped he didn't think I was dumb. But then again, I didn't care and just prayed that he had something to offer. Everyone I've met with tried to holler at me, women too. I thought he would be decent to work with because Lori recommended him, and she always wanted the best for me.

I locked my phone and took my heels off as I staggered to my front door.

I was a drunk woman.

CHAPTER 2

Oh, wait, that was you!

My phone chimed loudly, the sun beamed directly into my face, and birds chirped louder in my ear than my phone chimed.

I woke up from a drunken sleep on the concrete right in front of my door. I vowed never to drink again from that day on. Thank God nobody stumbled across me; that would've been the real problem. Not so much as someone hurting me, but me being the laughing stock of my community.

My phone rang for about five minutes before I found it laid between two tree shrubs. My head felt like a marching band was playing at a college football game on my temple. That headache must have happened when I fell into the shrubs and rolled over onto the concrete. I later found out once I looked at my security camera footage later that day. I looked at my front door window, and my hair was full of leaves. My freshly done lace front wig took a loss too. What a wild night?

I grabbed my keys that hid between my two flowerpots near the front door with one hand and finally answered my phone with the other. "Hello?"

"Damn, finally, I was just callin' to see if you made it home safely," she shouted.

"Lori?" I could barely hear her. My main focus was to

walk straight and keep the phone as far away from my ear because Lori could really yell.

"Yes, It's Lori. Girl, are you drunk? The fuck?"

"Yeah, you can say that, and yes, I made it home safely."

It would've been a different story if she had asked if I actually made it in the house.

"Did you have fun?" Whenever I went out without her, she wanted to hear how bad it went or hoped that it went as bad as she wanted it.

"Girl, yeah, so much fun. I have to call and check on Maxine. I don't remember seein' her when I left."

"Well, did she try to call you?" Lori loved to have something awful to happen to hold over Maxine's head. That would've made her day. Either way, it was bound to be some heat whenever Lori saw her.

I grabbed my heels and purse and went inside. "I don't know, let me check my phone for some messages." I flipped my wild, branch filled hair out of my face and scanned my text and call log. "No, I don't see anything from her."

"Told you that bitch is not your friend. I don't know why you keep hanging with her anyway," she blurted.

I walked over to the island and plugged my coffee maker into the socket. I grabbed a K-Cup Pod. "Yeah, yeah, what time is it anyway?"

I turned my head toward my rhinestone clock on my wall. It didn't work, but it was cute, though.

"It's...umm...eight O'clock," Lori said. "Why, what's going—"

"Oh, shoot, Cole." I panicked. I couldn't miss that meeting. He might have been the person I needed to move ahead and get what I need to get started finally. Like done now!

"Cole... what...is he there?"
"No, I have to meet him. I'll call you later. Bye."
Click.

I raced upstairs, grabbed clothes out of my closet, and threw them everywhere, looking for the perfect thing to wear. I didn't want to be underdressed, and I didn't want to be overdressed. I finally decided to put on my white woven cami and high waist black slacks. My pants legs touched the floor. That was one of my favorite outfits. The same outfit I wore to my law school interview. It felt like a glove on my body. It gripped my curves in all the right areas. I looked hella decent in it. They smelled like I just got them out a fabric softener filled dryer. I grabbed my black stilettos that I didn't wear often. They were my lucky stilettos. Maybe he would lower the price once he sees how nice I looked. I unglued my lace front and took down my twist that I hid underneath.

On my way out of the door, I grabbed an apple and my business folder from the kitchen table along with my coffee. "Marshall," I yelled. I waited for a reply, and there wasn't one. I ran out of the house and jumped into my BMW and sped off into the street, bumping one of my favorite songs, "Hot Girl Summer" by Megan thee Stallion ft Nicki Minaj and Ty Dolla $ign. I was breaking my back so hard driving. I lost control of the wheel and damn near ran over a kid and his dog. "I'm sorry," I yelled over my shoulder out of the window.

After I valet parked, I grabbed my phone from the cup holder and texted Cole on my way to the coffee shop's front door.

Hey Cole, I am here. I have on a white cami and black slacks.
I waited anxiously off to the side of the entrance.
Okay, I'm here too. I have already gotten us a table. I'll come

to get you.

I never really noticed how beautiful Rosettes really was on the outside. I stared at myself through the window of the perfect tan constructed building. I noticed that one of the straps from my cami was slightly crooked. To look less revealing, I pulled the strap over and pulled the front of my shirt above my breast's crease. I lined up my eyeliner with the side of my finger using my hand mirror that I quickly grabbed from my purse. My eyes were gray that day.

Someone tapped my shoulder. My smile became so sharp it could cut a watermelon in half. I turned, and my face dropped with disbelief. I'll be damned. It was the idiot in the black Infiniti truck that cut me off the day before. I couldn't believe the guy that I was not trying to give attention to would be getting my attention anyway, maybe even my money. It's funny how life works.

"Hello, my name is Cole." He extended his hand toward mine. He was much taller than I was, by a few inches—the average size for a man. Coincidently our eyes were the same color. I didn't get a good look at him the first time. He was a'ight. I was lyin' to myself. He was fione.

"Hi, My name is Ronnie." I extended my hand, hoping that our hands wouldn't link. But he assured that our hands connected with a firm handshake.

"Shall we go inside?" He gripped the door handle, stepped off to the side, and let me lead the way into the coffee shop.

"Yes, we shall." I walked through them. I wanted to turn around, go back home, call Lori, and tell her how I would beat her up to for giving me that idiots number. But I gave him a chance.

We walked over to our table. The whiff of him smelled

very masculine and clean. He pulled my chair from the table so that I could have a seat.

Before he could get to his side of the table to position himself, he began to talk with that powerful masculine voice. "So, Lori tells me that you are looking to start your own firm. Is that right?" He stared me in my eyes and not at my breast.

"Yes, that is correct. I am looking to get it up and running within another years timeframe."

"Can I ask what made you want to open your firm?" He grabbed his napkin off the table and laid it across his legs.

"Are you sure you have time to listen?"

"Yes, that is what I am here for." He placed his hands on the table and interlocked his fingers.

"Well, back in college, I was dating this guy, and he was on the football team. He broke his arm and had to take steroids. He became addicted to them and got kicked off the team. He became very depressed and went to the doctor. The doctor diagnosed him with bipolar depression. In conclusion, he was misdiagnosed because of a doctor's negligence on the job, and that's when I decided to become a Malpractice Lawyer. Moving forward, I am tired of working for someone else, and I want to own my establishment. I want to be like the Scotts & Williams, LLC. You know the huge firm in New York City, right?"

"Yes, I know what firm you are talking about. They are an okay company. We can get you up there on their level. That's no problem, but if you don't mind me asking, whatever happened to the guy you were dating?" His strong eye contact showed he was really interested.

"I am married to him. Going on ten years together with two years of marriage."

"Happy ending," he said, a little salty. "But on another

note, I am the guy for the job. I've been doing this for about four years. I've had over hundreds of clients. They have been in different areas. No one has ever come to me to start a firm, but believe me, I am your guy. If you need any references, please let me—"

"If Lori says you are good. Then you are good. My cousin wouldn't send me off," I asserted.

"Okay, we are good then. I work in public relations, marketing, and investments. I also have some skills in real estate. If I don't have the answers, I have my resources. Do you have any questions so far?"

"Yes, I actually do. Can you find out about different areas of availability somewhere close to the city? Do you think that would be a great location?"

"Yes, it could be. At the same time, many people are looking for your services, and we must make sure you have easy access to your clients. You don't want them to have any more added stress. I'll try to find you an area where you can invest in as well."

"Whoa...whoa...whoa, now you are speaking my language." It was worth giving him my time so far. I hoped I didn't regret it.

"Well, that's good to know," he continued. "You can have one business pay for your other businesses. I'll contact my close friend to look into different commercial properties. I'll work on your marketing strategies. Next meeting, I'll have a portfolio together for you to look over."

"Are you trying to get over on me?"

"Naw, this is real shi-" he caught himself before he said anymore. He unlocked his hands and placed them on his lap.

"I'll let that little slip-up slide. Don't worry." I didn't

hold that against him. I just knew then that I wouldn't be working with a tight-ass.

"Thank you. I appreciate it." He grinned and I stared at his smile.

"Sounds good then." The waitress brought my iced coffee with extra milk. "Thank you." I slid her a tip.

"Wow, they just bring your stuff on over, huh?" he said, looking at me and then at the waitress.

"Can you bring him one too?" I asked the waitress.

"They sure do. Lori and I have been coming here for years," I said to Cole.

Our waitress walked off with a smile.

"Oh, okay, cool. You know you can call me whenever you like, night and day. I am here to help you with whatever you need," he said with a smile. His teeth lined up perfectly. They looked real. A lot of people I knew loved getting veneers. I guess that's why I couldn't keep my eyes off of his matured styled looking veneers.

"Okay, sounds like a plan." I smiled back.

"You have a beautiful smile. Might I add." Cole glared at me.

"Why, thank you." I smiled again, hoping the discount would be a big one.

"I have a question for you, Ronnie."

"Yes, what is it." I took a sip of my delicious coffee and crossed one leg over the other.

"Do I look familiar to you?" He said with a straight face.

"No, you don't." I lied. "Should you?"

"Really?" he chuckled.

"Did we go to school together or something?" I took another sip of coffee and crossed my legs at the ankles.

The waitress brought him an iced coffee.

"C'mon, stop playing. Now I know you remember me.

Think long and hard." He turned his head sideways in an act to get me to picture how I would've remembered how he looked when I first saw him.

"No, I have no idea." I lied, with confidence. I held my head high.

"Just yesterday afternoon, I was on the side of you trying to get your attention."

He wasn't a tight-ass, but he was starting to act like a jackass and I honestly wanted to forget that ever happened. And I did forget that it even happened. I was in my moment. My moment of happiness.

"Huh?" I stared up and over his shoulder pretending to draw back a memory of him. "Ohhhhh, yeahhh, that was... that was you, huh? The one who tried to cause an accident. Yeah, now I remember. Yes, you do look familiar."

"I was not trying to cause an accident. That was you, and since you will possibly be my new client, I won't report you."

"Ha-ha-ha. Report me, huh?"

"Yes, report you,' he laughed. "But like I said...now that you are a client, I will not only hold back from reporting you, but I will keep it very professional. Plus, I now know that you are married."

"Why, thank you. I would appreciate that."

"But, I am going to head on out now and take care of some business, and if there is anything else you need, you can give me a call. For Lori's cousin, it's a 24-hour service. Text or call me when you want to set up the next meeting." He put a few dollars on the table for the bill.

"I'll be calling you soon. I want to get this ball on the roll. Take care." We shook hands, and he got up from the table and left. I walked over to the window seats and called Lori to fill her in on what Cole and I just talked about while I enjoyed the rest of my iced coffee.

I rushed home after my last sip of coffee. I was so thrilled that I wanted to tell Marshall immediately once I saw him. I walked through the door. It was just as quiet as it was when I first left that morning.

"Marshalllll." No answer. "Marshallll," I yelled louder and louder.

It was a good thing he wasn't there yet; I went to our room and grabbed my black laced corset and matching thong. I raced to the shower and washed my body from my head to my toes, not once, not twice, but five times. I wanted to make sure it would be a great night, which started with a fresh ass. I also hoped that he would walk in while I was in the shower so that we could have blissful sex.

I was ecstatic from my meeting with Cole that I thought it would be an excellent time to make a baby. If I was not already pregnant, we were getting pregnant that night. I put on my sexy lingerie and all-black heels.

Marshall had not made it back yet, so I started on dinner. I made his favorite meal. He loved steak with garlic bread, baked potatoes, and corn on the cob. The door slammed. I saw him making his way into the kitchen. I stood ready for him to wrap his arms around me and make love to me on our kitchen island.

"Hey, Babe. How was your day? I have some exciting news. Things are moving forward." I walked towards him for a kiss.

"What the fuck is that smell?" He grabbed my arm and shoved me off to the side and kept walking past me. That was nowhere near what I expected.

"What do you mean, what's that smell? It's the smell of your favorite dinner, Duh!"

"I don't like that shit," he said as he threw his Gucci backpack down on the kitchen island.

He always loved the smell of his favorite dinner. I've cooked that meal a dozen times and the same way every time. He said I cooked it better than the Steak House. What a difference a day made.

"What do you mean you don't like that shit? You love this shit." I walked over to the stove and turned it off.

"Not today, not tomorrow, not no other time. I am going to bed. I don't feel like this shit today." Marshall walked past me, and I followed to comfort him. "I am going to bed by myself," he said over his shoulder.

"Okay, I hope you feel better." I flipped him the bird. I couldn't understand his behavior. Yesterday he was so lovey-dovey, now he is upset. He acted as if he were bipolar. We had been doing so well. One day he was bustin' in me and the next I wanted to bust him in the head.

When I got to the room, Marshall was on his phone playing a basketball game. I got into bed and put my feet under his legs. He brushed my feet from under him. I didn't even get mad. I was too happy, and I wasn't going to let him get me angry over something I knew nothing about. So, I took the rejection and got a good night's rest.

When I woke up, Marshall had already left. I remembered waking up through the night to use the bathroom and to get a snack, but I couldn't recall what time he might've left. I glanced at the time, and it was nine in the morning, two days later. I couldn't believe I slept in for two days without doing anything. I didn't even text or call him to figure him out. He let me sleep for two days without a hello or a kiss. That was one of the weirdest things I've dealt with in a long time. But, I didn't dwell on it. I set some time aside for myself and focused on researching more about my future firm.

I walked into the bank and instantly got a seat with an agent. She checked my records to find out how much I would prequalify for. I thought about Marshall and how he could be so unconcerned about me starting my firm. He had not asked me one question about the process, how it was going, or did I even need anything. Between Marshall's income and mine, I made all the money. That's how our mortgage and utilities got paid and how we kept food in the house. He was only able to pay his bills from the money left over from his lawsuit. He hadn't put anything into that house. He put most of his time into other females. If he had put most of his time into our home and no other females. We would've probably already had a few babies.

He hadn't thought about facts. If I had moved out that motherfucking house, how would he have been able to afford it, but you know what, that was probably all that he thought about. He knew he was about to become a certified pharmacist, and he would then have enough money to be on his own. The only thing that would probably make him stay with me after he started making his own money would be our baby.

Bzzz...bzzz...buzz. Lori's name lit up in the display. I ignored it. I had some things to think about, and I couldn't tell Lori. She would go nuts.

"So, Miss Lawson. You would qualify for $750,000. Would you like to proceed now?" The agent slid me the printout.

"Yes, I would love to proceed."

"Well, I'll send your paperwork through, and you'll hear back from me anywhere between 3 to 5 business days."

"Okay, that's fine with me."

"Can you sign here?" She handed me a pen.

Once I left the bank. I texted Cole.

Hey Cole, I just came from the bank and have been approved for a nice amount of money. I have to wait at least 3-5 business days for the final numbers, but we are getting this on a roll.

Hello Mrs. Valentine. Sounds like a plan. I'll contact my realtor and tell her to keep her eyes open.

Okay, thanks a lot Cole. I'll be in touch.

Okay, and make sure to keep my updated on everything.

I am a businesswoman!

CHAPTER 3

HER

I got home, and Marshall was still not there. I hadn't seen him for days. I called his phone at least five times, and he didn't answer, nor did he call me back. I checked his social media sites, and he hadn't posted in a couple of hours. No signs of anything serious happening.

I called Maxine in hopes that she heard from him.

"Hello?"

"Yeah, Maxine...Ummm... Have you heard from Marshall?" My forearm laid across my abdomen and my hand cuffed my side.

"Yes, I talked to him about an hour or two ago."

"Did he seem to be okay?"

"He seemed to be fine. He was on his way home," she said with not a worry in the world.

'He seemed to be fine' could've meant when she talked to him, he didn't have any emotion. Which could've meant he was feeling better and we could have a better evening.

"Okay, then. Let me know if you hear from him."

"Don't worry, girl. He will be there soon."

Click.

He was fine. I reassured myself and even laughed a little. He'd stayed out before, but he'd always answer my calls.

I jumped in the shower and hoped he had joined me soon. We used to fuck in the shower like almost every night. He would always manage to walk in right in the middle of me washing up. I made sure I started between my legs because he loved to demolish my pussy first. I finished up in the shower and made my way into our bedroom. He still hadn't come in. I put on my booty shorts and a tank top because I was still hot from my steamed shower. My nipples poked out, and you could see the print through my shirt. I wanted to look extra ready when he walked through the door.

I started preparing dinner on our white kitchen counter as I waited for him to walk through the door. I thought I'd give it another try. This time I was going to cook something fast and straightforward. The aroma in the kitchen was fresh. My pasta was boiling. My fresh tomatoes, diced onion, garlic, basil, oregano, bay leaves, parsley, and last but not least, sea salt was ready to be added to my chicken breast. It smelled so good in the kitchen; there was no way anything could have gone wrong. I just wanted to talk to him about starting my firm and trying to get pregnant.

In the middle of stirring my pasta, I remembered that I had a track my friend's app on my phone. I put it on his phone a while ago. I was pretty sure he hadn't seen it. I grabbed my phone and logged in. I got a few password and username do not match, but when I finally got in, the green button showed he was at his school.

Maybe he lost his phone.
Did someone steal it?
Maybe he got hurt, and no one had discovered him.

I drove my car directly to where the green bubble took me. I pulled up in front of a newly rehabbed three-story building with a red butterfly roof. There was a big sign that said Graysville Study Hall.

I paused before jumping out of my car. My heart skipped a beat, several beats at the sight of Marshall walking with some girl. I did not approach him. Instead, I kept an eye on him. I had known him to have girls as friends, but I knew all the ones he did have. Her body shape didn't match any of the girls he had previously introduced me to. I could see them both from across the courtyard. She was medium built with wide hips; her frame was decent. I tried to get a better view, but the trees were blocking the garden street lights. I couldn't make out what the girl looked like because she wore a black jogging suit with the hood flipped over her head.

It was around eighty to ninety degrees. Why did she have on a jogging suit, anyway? She looked crazy. Big ass jogging suit just hanging off her.

No matter how dark it was though, I knew that it was Marshall with her. I knew that swagger walk from anywhere. They walked over to his car, and he opened the door. This bitch hasn't opened the door for me in forever and a fucking day. In the distance, there was an outburst of laughter. The bitch turned into a comedian overnight. Yeah, fuck-ing right. Well, okay, I was being a hater. Marshall was funny.

My car was so close to his cars bumper. I mean, I really followed them very carefully. I wasn't sure what I would do if he noticed me. The only thing that was sure of was to stay close and lay low. The yellow light turned red and I slammed on the breaks. I had to slow it down, relax, and pay attention before I got caught.

I called his phone, and he didn't answer. He was having the time of his life because he hadn't recognized his wife had been following him for miles. I was never sucking his motherfucking dick again.

They pulled up to a restaurant. Red carpet rolled across the seventeen-step staircase. There were big green bushes that aligned on each side of the steps. The beautiful building lit throughout with lights and expensive suits. Marshall spent some money, money on her. His little thirst bucket ass should've been taking me out and celebrating with me, but instead he pampered a slow motherfucker who walked into one of the most beautiful restaurants in the city with a jogging suit on. He sure knew how to pick them.

The valet driver walked up to his car. Marshall gave the driver his keys before he ran around to the other side of the car and opened the door for her. Damn, it was really like that. It seemed like he was doing everything he could to get some ass. When she got out of the car she had a bouquet of fucking red roses. He grabbed her hand and helped her up the stairs. The greeter met them at the door.

It took everything out of me to not follow them into the resturant. My body temperature was hotter than Texas. My temples throbbed and were going to burst. My fingers ached. I rubbed my hands together to get a grip on myself. I raised my foot to the window but stopped before I could extend it to kick my front window out. I placed my foot back down on the floor.

I followed the valet driver to the parking lot. The driver jumped out and walked away. I lurked over to Marshalls red Camaro and picked up a brick aimed at the passenger side window. I looked in the backseat, and my Gucci duffle bag and jacket laid under the seat. It would have been just my luck to have broken his windows, and somebody steals my shit out of his car. Instead, I ran back to the car and searched through my purse for my travel-sized wine opener. I ran back to the side of his car, pierced his tires, flattening them.

I laughed while joyful tears ran down my face. I pulled on the doorknob of my car, and I couldn't get it opened. I wiped the tears from my eyes and noticed I wasn't standing at my car after all. I jumped into *my* vehicle and darted off so fast into ongoing traffic. I almost caused an accident. I didn't care, though, because I was overjoyed. My music blasted. I got more cheerful when little drops of rain hit my windshield. It rarely rained in that part of town. I guess God was on my side that night. It started to rain harder, and I drove into my happiness. Marshall was going to have a hard time getting his tire together in the rain, and he better not had called me looking for a way to get home.

I finally got back home and turned my music on in my kitchen. I could barely function without my music. I prepared my pasta. A few hours later, Marshall walked and slammed the front door. I could see everything through our floor to ceiling windows. He was so fumed. I was afraid if he came into the kitchen, he would blow up like a ticking time bomb. I turned back toward the stove to avoid any confrontation. I vaguely turned and glanced at him, he tried to hide his muddy white shirt in the coat closet. He looked like he had a hard time changing his tire after all.

I turned fully facing the stove when I saw him walking toward the kitchen.

"What's wrong with you?" My face ached, I tried so hard to hold in my laughter.

"Man, look, I don't want to talk about it," he angrily replied as he walked toward the kitchen island for a seat.

I stirred my noodles, and then turned the heat down. "No baby, we need to talk about whatever it is that is bothering you," I said over my shoulder. I sounded genuinely concerned, but of course I wasn't. I turned around toward him and made eye contact. While I stared at him, I pictured him struggling to change his tire out in the rain.

"What the hell is so funny?"

I shook my head side to side. "Nothing."

"You know what." He shook his head. "There is something on my mind." He got up from his seat and fixed him a drink.

"Okay, what is it that you need to talk about?"

"Why in the hell did you tell Maxine we can't get pregnant?" He gulped down some brown liquor. "She told my mom, and they called me on three-way, trying to get the whole story. They ass don't need to know what's going on in this damn house. You know my mom, your mom, and other people always askin' 'when are you guys going to have a baby. Your babies will be so adorable.' You know how embarrassing and unsettling that is to hear. We've been hearing that for the last two years."

"Well, I understand your anger, but—"

"There is no but. We are trying, and now we can't have the babies they are always talkin' about."

He was trying to put his anger on me. Here was this cheating dog who now wanted to be mad at me about talking to his sister. The one he encouraged me to speak to in the first place. That was most definitely not the problem. But I knew one thing though; he was gone learn that day to not come at me on no bullshit.

He walked over to the corner where my bluetooth

speaker was. "Turn this down."

I walked over to the Bluetooth speaker and turned the music up, but not too loud, I needed him to hear everything that was about to fly out of my mouth. "I don't know who you think you are to come in this motherfucking house after not answering your got damn phone all day and talk to me like I am some bitch on the streets. I can tell whoever...whatever the fuck I want. Fuck you!"

"Whatever Ronn—"

"You not gone come in here on bullshit. Period!" I grabbed the paprika off the island and threw some at his face. He leaned to the side like he was in the matrix, and the paprika missed him. I was somewhat glad it missed him. I just tried to scare his ass. "You have been tripping the last couple of days."

"Really? We throwing shit now?" he slid all of my sea-seasoning and cooking utensils off the island onto the floor. "You tell people what I want you to tell them. Not what you think you should tell them. Especially my business. Tripping or not."

"Well, there's where we have a problem. It's not just your business, fool. It's our business!"

"Look, Ronnie."

"Oh, now we are using government names, huh? Well, Look here, Marshall. I advise you to go back to yo bitch house. That's where you need to be right now. Before things get uglier than what they already are."

"What the hell are you talking about?" he said, walking toward me.

"You know what the hell I am talking about. Go back to yo bitch because right now is not the time to be fucking with me," I repeated. "But before you leave. PICK MY SHIT UP OFF THE MOTHER-FUCKING FLOOR, YOU

FOOL!" I threw my spoon on the island, it bounced off, and it almost hit him. "Take those problems back to where you came from," I yelled over my shoulder. "Acting like you mad because I talked to your sister about our fertility problems," I mumbled as I continued to walk up the stairs.

When I got to our room, I knocked everything over on our nightstand when I grabbed the remote. The picture of Marshall and I was the first thing to drop to the floor. I even broke my favorite watch that my mom gotten me for my graduation. I sat at the end of our bed for a while. To calm down, I decided to watch my favorite comedian. I knew for sure he would take my mind off all the bull-shit. I realized I didn't grab my champagne from in the fridge downstairs. I couldn't watch television at a time like that without getting a little tipsy. I walked past the guest room, where I saw Marshall getting ready for bed.

"Why are you still here?" I stuck my head through the door. "Huh?"

His back faced me and without saying a word or even looking at me, he cut the lamp off. "Don't turn off shit in here. You don't pay no damn bills." I slammed the door shut.

My champagne was nice and cold when I grabbed it from the fridge. I noticed he cleaned up everything. The garbage was almost full. I should've told his mad ass to take out the trash, but I decided to let him play the vic-tim and not worry about anything like I always do.

I walked past the guest room and the door was still shut. He didn't know that I installed cameras in the guest room not long before he had to spend the night there. I didn't install them for cheating purposes. I had them set up to keep an eye on his parents when they came to stay.

Every time they came to visit, a few of my champagne bottles would come up missing. I'd ask them what
happened to my champagne, and everyone would act all
Cher Horowitz. So, I set up cameras to catch a motherfucker. Marshall called me boujee because I enjoyed me
some champagne to wind down while other women enjoyed drinking wine, so 'boujee' was my middle name.

I laid in my memory foam bed with my white king
size woven comforter laid across me. I watched reruns of
Martin. The show *Martin* was so funny to me and took my
mind off of the nonsense that was going on. I laid down
in my bed, drunk my champagne out of the bottle, and
tried to enjoy the rest of my night. I kicked my legs up and
down on the bed and made loud noises so Marshall could
hear me. I laughed and snorted. I didn't even snort on the
regular, but I wanted him to get the point that our bed
didn't miss him in it. I looked at the wireless monitor,
and I saw Marshall laying in the dark with his phone in
his hand. He smiled and he was so entertained. I saw the
blanket motioning in an up and down direction where
he dick was. Was the fool masturbating? I should've gone
in there and knocked down the damn door but, I kept
my cool. I had to find out the name of that bitch he was
cheating on me with.

I grabbed my phone from the floor, and I texted Lori. I
didn't want to tell her what's going on through text messages. I didn't want to hear her mouth.

Hey cousin, meet me at rosettes for brunch tomorrow. Before I could wait for a response, I fell asleep. Champagne
did it for me.

Riiinggg. My head poun-ded. I turned over to turn my
alarm off, and an empty bottle of champagne laid peace-

fully by my side. I couldn't believe I drank damn near the whole bottle. Anxious to find a bouquet of red roses on my nightstand I turned toward it. There was nothing; there were no roses. Marshall would give me flowers every time he and I got into a big argument. No matter what the situation was, I had roses—lots of them.

Me not getting roses reminded me of that night his new girl had a bouquet of roses. He must have made her mad. After putting the puzzle together, my day started crushed, knowing in a blink of an eye, my feelings didn't matter anymore. I checked my phone to see if I had a response from Lori.

What time???

Hellooooo?

Are you there?

I tried to call bish. Are you alive? Text me tomorrow if you are alive.

Lori was so funny. I texted her back.

Sorry bout that. I fell asleep. Yes, I am alive. Meet me there at one o'clock. I stretched so hard I almost broke my back. That champagne did it to me. Felt like I slept for days.

Text tone

Okay, see you then, and next time, call me when you are falling asleep, DAMN!

Okay, DAMN! I got up, and I stretched some more. I couldn't believe that I didn't have any flowers waiting for me on the nightstand. Double blow to the face.

I walked past the guest room on my way to the kitchen. I noticed that Marshall had already left. The bed had been made with clean sheets. He probably didn't want to hear my mouth again. He must have left out early to groom himself for his graduation reception that night. I prepared my coffee while I confirmed my doctor's appointment that I dreaded going to after the night I had.

"Hello, this is Carter Medical Group. My name is Rachel. How can I help you?"

I walked over to the coffee maker and loaded it with a roasted black flavored k cup. "Hey girl, this is Ronnie. My appointment is today, right?"

"Hey, Boo." Indistinct typing in the background. "Yes, it is here at this facility at nine o'clock."

I looked down at my wristwatch to check the time. The bezel laid on the inner part of my wrist. "Okay, girl, I will see you in a few." I unplugged my coffee maker and let the cord fall to the table.

In the middle of me adding cream and sugar to my coffee

Text tone.

Cole's name lit up in the display.

I have the portfolio ready. Let me know when you want to meet to go over all the details.

Okay. I'll let you know as soon as possible. I took a sip of my coffee.

Okay. That's fine. Thanks for your time.

I poured the rest of the coffee I had left in my travel cup and drunk it on my way my appointment.

"Ronnie Lawson," the nurse shouted and browsed the crowd. She was a cheerful nurse that stood about 5'9" with gorgeous long hair.

"Here I am." I got up from my seat and followed her to the room.

"Is this your date of birth?" She showed me the urine cup label.

"Yes, that's correct."

"Can you give me some urine in the cup and place it in

room 304c?" she instructed.

Everyone was always friendly. I couldn't have imagine going anywhere else for care. I greeted everyone as I slowly walked to the bathroom. There were enough nurses to catch me before falling out on the ground if I found out I were pregnant. Once I got in the bathroom, I washed my hands, sat slightly above the seat, and place the cup right under me. I ended up peeing all over myself. It was nothing new. My thighs and ass were too big to try to catch pee in that little ass cup.

I walked down the hall to room 304c and placed the cup in the room.

"Follow me," a shrill voice behind me ordered. When we got to the chilled room, the nurse handed me a thin white gown. "Undress and put this on. The doctor will be right with you. "

"Hi Mrs. Valentine." The doctor walked in as the nurse left out.

"Hi. Doctor Reese," I greeted with a smile which she couldn't see because she stood behind the curtain that separated the doctors from the patients.

"How have you been?" She walked from behind the curtain over to the automatic hands-free hand sanitizer dispenser. I could see her, but she didn't look my way.

"I've been doing great. How about yourself?" I continued to get undressed.

"I've been doing pretty good myself." She nodded her head up and down. "I can't complain. How is Marshall?"

"That's good to hear and he is okay." I put my gown on and sat on the exam table.

"So, besides your annual checkup, are there anything other concerns you may have today?" She walked over to where I sat and stood in front of me.

"Yes, as a matter of fact I do, Doctor Reese. I wanted to know if you could check my urine. I've been famished and sleepy a lot lately."

"Have you been eating enough? Have you been drinking enough fluids? Have you been getting the proper rest?

"Yes, I have." I nodded my head up and down.

"Okay, when was your last period?" She grabbed my patient chart and looked over it.

"I'm not even sure."

"Well," she sounded unconcerned. "I've already checked your urine, and it came back negative for both pregnancy and urinary tract infection. So maybe your period is coming soon."

I started to feel better already. Thank God I was not pregnant by that sneaky foul ass dog ass fool. I didn't know what I would do if I was.

She continued, "I want you to keep track of your period from now on." She placed the chart on the desk. "So, with your annual checkup, I will check your pelvis, give you a pap smear, and a breast exam."

I hated that damn pap smear part of the visit. It was like trying to get a cat to take a bath.

"I will check for any other infections. When your results come in, you will get a call from the office if anything comes back abnormal. I will have some bloodwork drawn up for you. So, you can go straight to the lab when you leave here," she instructed.

I couldn't deal with the lab. I had to deal with other things like finding out why I didn't get any flowers and his side chick did. I was on a roller coaster full of emotions. Where did I go wrong? I thought things were perfect.

She walked over to the side of me. She brought her hand through the back of my gown. Her hands were cold when she rubbed them up and around my breast before I heard the hurtful words, "Now lay back and spread your legs. Place your feet in the stirrups."

I seriously tried to find ways to make that process a little easier for myself. But the part with me laying down on my back with my legs spread out like a cat in heat never helped make anything easier. Not to mention, I had to be half ass naked, and the room was always colder than a motherfucker. She stuck this big ass plastic tube in my vagina, and it hurt like hell. Although Marshall's dick was much bigger than that, pap smear never served me any pleasure.

She grabbed the speculum, then inserted it into the vagina and slightly opened it. My toes clenched the whole time. I tried to relax my vagina muscles, but I also tried to hold a fart inside. The visit went left.

"I am almost finished. I just have to scrap the cells," the doctor said.

"Take your time." My breathy voice meant hurry up.

"All done." She slid back from between legs.

"Thank God."

"Now, the next part."

Uhh oh.

She walked over to her desk, and I eased the fart out. It was a small burst of wind. It didn't smell too bad, either. Well, to me, it didn't. She walked back over to me and looked faint. She dipped her fingers in and out of me faster than you can say the letter A. She rolled back in her chair and sputtered. "Welp, that's it. You can pick up your bloodwork from the referral desk. See you back in a year." She stood by the door and pulled on the doorknob. I thought I saw a tear in one of her eyes. She gasped for air. "Till we get the results back from the lab, try to eat and

sleep more and see if you see a change. Have a good one."
She vanished from the room faster than a superhero.

Well, that ended well for me. I sat up, and the waft of
my fart changed my mind. The fart was one of its kind—
that damn coffee.

Text tone. Lori name lit up in the display.

Don't be late again, bish!!!!! I mean it.

Ha-Ha-Ha. On my way now, and I am not lying.

I continued to put on my clothes.

Doing seventy in a fifty-five-mph zone, I got stopped
by a red light. There were a lot of people out enjoying
their day. My heart ached, and I wanted a piece of happiness, even if it were small. People walked gleefully down
the streets. This one group of people reminded me of
Marshall and me. The only difference between them and
us were they looked happy and had two children along-
side them. Well, that happened to be a huge difference.
We were not happy together, nor did we have children.

Couples cuddled each other. The amount of love for
one another showed in their mannerisms, smiles, and fa-
cial expressions. The kids smiled while they rode their
bikes. Those smiles brought out a ray of sunshine for me.
Those smiles stitched my heart together. They stepped
off the curb, the man slapped the woman on the butt and
kissed her on the lips. The crossing guard smiled at the
couple, and the couple smiled back. The woman grabbed
and held her man's butt. Why couldn't I have that happy
grabbing ass life?!

Honk. Hoonnnk.

I looked through my review mirror at the traffic I had
at a halt. I sped off.

When I got to the restaurant, I walked over to Lori. Her

eyes pierced through me. She looked concerned. "What's wrong with you?" she asked.

"Nothing, long day." I lied.

"Nah, something is wrong. You wanted to meet. So, you better tell me before I raise hell in here," she raised her voice as if she were my mother.

"Everything is fine. I just wanted to see you. I've been so busy lately. I just wanted to catch up." I pulled my seat from the table and flopped down.

"Tell me because I don't want to have to whoop someone's ass today," she said with aggression.

I laid my purse on the table after I sat down. I wanted to tell Lori so badly about what happened last night, but I didn't want to look like a fool again. "No, you don't have to whoop anyone's ass today," I giggled. "Everything is okay." I lied. I had to tell her about the pregnancy. Lori could always detect my pain. "Well, I just left my doctors appoint—"

You ain't tell me about no damn doctors' appointment." She frowned. "You know I would've gone with you. Did Marshall go?"

"No. I went alone. I didn t tell him I had an appointment either." I rested my cheek into the palm of my right hand. My left arm laid across my abdomen. "I am tired of having all these false results, and that would only make things worse."

"What do you mean worst?"

"Like, make him feel some type of way because we can't get pregnant."

"Oh, girl fuck him. This is about you." She fanned her hand like she was dismissing his feelings.

"But other than that, I am fine.' That cheating shit ate me alive, but I couldn't tell Lori because she would've gotten super mad and turned into inspector gadget. I needed to handle that situation on my own.

Lori whispered, "Look." She nodded her head in the direction behind me.

I turned around, and it was Maxine. She looked like she was with that girl I was dancing with at the yacht party.

Was that why the bitch didn't call me to check on me?! Too busy making new friends.

Lori yelled, "Maxine, Hey girl." Lori was always messy. She was still ready to start stuff with her. No matter the situation.

Maxine walked over to our table. The girl from the yacht party stood at the front, speaking to the waitress at the takeout counter.

"Girl, what's going on? I haven't seen you in a while. How have you been? Have you been good, or what?" Ron said you all went out to a yacht party, and she mentioned you didn't call to see if she got home," Lori said in an aggressive tone.

"Wait, I did talk to her yesterday. Sorry, I didn't call you to see if you made it safe, but I walked you to your car, and you said you were okay. I guess you weren't okay because you couldn't remember that."

"Oh, yeahhh, I forgot. You sure did. Right after getting handed the keys from the valet drivers." I didn't feel like talking about that at the moment. To me, the issue had already been handled and buried. But Lori could never let Maxine slide, and you can't tell a grown woman what to do.

"Yes, I was there. I even made sure I tipped the valet." she admitted to Lori.

"See, I told you, Lori. There was nothing to worry about."

Lori rolled her eyes.

"Can I talk to you for a minute Maxine? I have to talk to you about something really quick." Although she was Marshall's sister and she could lie, I still took the chance to speak with her about his cheating. I was sure she could tell me something about what had been going on with Marshall lately. We walked toward the corner by the bathroom. I could see the girl from the yacht party looking around the restaurant. I wasn't sure if she was looking for Maxine, but I wasn't going to tell Maxine either way. I needed Maxine's full attention.

"What do you need to talk to her about?" Lori yelled.

I grabbed Maxine's arm and walked her further into the corner by the restroom. "Your brother is cheating on me." I blurted out.

"Wow...what?" Her eyes widened.

"He is cheating on me," I repeated.

"Damn, Ronnie. You have to give me a heads up. You can't just blurt out something like that."

"Yeah, well. It's something that I need answers to."

"I am sorry, so sorry Ronnie."

"So, you knew about this?"

"Hell nah Ronnie. The last time he tried to bring another girl around mom and me, mom flipped out on him. You know momma is not having none of that cheating stuff after my dad cheated on her. Momma Valentine does not play that.

"That's true. I'm just concerned. I thought everything was good, and then here we are again."

"You know momma don't take no shit. Marshall's ass was sick from sadness when momma put him in his place."

"That doesn't mean he stopped cheating tho; that just

means he stopped trying to bring the girls around you two."

"Girl, he is so disrespectful, and we know who he gets it from. I am so sorry, Ronnie." She hugged me so tight that it could have killed a bear.

"How did you and ole girl become friends?" I asked her curiously.

"Girl, who?" She looked around with an arch in her eyebrow.

"The one from the party. I saw you over by the takeout together."

"Ooooh her." She looked in the direction of the takeout counter. "We are not friends. We just so happened to run into each other at the door. We said hi to each other and kept it moving. That's your friend, remember?!" she laughed.

"Ha-Ha. She is not my friend. She cool, though. But, I just thought you all were kicking it together now."

"Nah, I thought you all were kicking it together. Y'all was so turnt up at that damn party. I thought that was your new best friend." I looked over to the takeout corner. The girl was gone.

"Ha-Ha-Ha. Nah, you know I don't fuck with people like that. I was fucked up. As you can tell when I didn't know you walked me to the car that day."

"Yeah, I did. So, stop telling Lori that I am doing you bogus."

"Maxine Valentine." The takeout waitress yelled for her to get her order.

She leaned in and gave me another bear hug. "But I love you, and I have to get on out of here. See you at the graduation."

Lori's eyes pierced through me, again. "Okay, now

what the hell was that about?" she said before I could even take my seat.

"What was what?"

"That..." She snapped her neck and pointed her finger towards Maxine.

"Nothing really, I was talking to her about the same thing I told you." I avoided eye contact with her.

"Then why in the hell you couldn't tell her when she was over here." She twisted and turned her neck with an attitude.

"Because you would've thrown your two cents in about what we were talking about. I wanted to talk and be the only one talking."

"Hmmm, that's because you know I am a human lie detector test, and I feel like you are lying to me or not telling me everything, but It's cool. I ain't gon trip about it. You better be lucky I love you because I'd throw this damn chair at you if I didn't. Anyway, what are you doing later?"

"It's Marshall's graduation reception this evening."

"Oh, okay. You don't tell me nothing anymore. That's something I would've known about a long time ago. But I am going to find out what's really going on soon enough."

I didn't think Lori cared about stuff like that. I still don't think she cared. Lori just wanted to know my every move. She didn't trust anyone. She tried to always be by my side. I felt terrible for not telling her the truth, but—

"Hellloooo." I was absent-minded. Lori waved her hands across my face trying to get my attention.

"Bish, I said that's something I would've known about a long time ago."

"It isn't that serious, Lori," I yelled. "The man won a settlement for a misdiagnosis for being prescribed the wrong medication from his doctor, he sued, got paid, decided to become a pharmacist, and now he is graduating. Nothing major."

"Damn, okay, then. You didn't have to say it like that. Something must be going on between you and Marshall, but I will not pry. I just know he probably wouldn't have made it this far if it wasn't for your love and support."

"Yup, I was very supportive. His parents set us up in a nice condo and asked me to take care of him since they lived far away. I was the only dumb ass girl who stayed with him when he got injured. The low key bitches didn't see a reason to stay and fuck him anymore."

"Through thick and thin before you even got married."

"My dumbass," I muttered.

"What did you say?"

"Nothing...nothing at all, girl." I looked down at my phone, if I didn't leave, I would be late. "Well, let me get out of here and go get ready for this reception."

Lori pulled money out of her purse. "You havin' a bad day. I got this. Have fun tonight, and don't overthink your infertility issues. I love you."

That was the last thing on my mind. I had bigger fish to fry. If she only knew how I really felt. "I love you too, I'll call you tomorrow." I walked around the tan square table and kissed her on the cheek.

"I'll be waiting." She smiled.

The valet pulled up with my car. He put the car keys in my hand. "Hello, Gorgeous."

I am glad he didn't call me ma'am. "Hello," I replied. He opened the door for me. I buckled myself in, turned my music up, and rode off in the evening skies.

I was a vulnerable woman!

CHAPTER 4

The Reception

T ext tone. Gale name lit up in the display. She called twice. She didn't leave a message, so it must not have been urgent. I pulled up to a red light. A couple walked out of a shopping mall. They looked so happy. *Beeeeep.* I looked in my rearview mirror; someone threw their hands up. I was holding up traffic again.

I pulled up to the stop sign that stood on the corner of our block. Marshall pulled out of the driveway. When I pulled in the driveway, I called his cell.

"Hello?" music blasted in the background. "Hold on... Now, I can hear you." The music disappeared from his background.

"Where are you going? I thought your reception was tonight. Did something change?"

"No, I am on my way to pick up the tickets from school. I'll swing that way once I get them.

"Should I start getting dressed?"

"Yes."

"Okay then. See you when you get back."

Click.

There was an envelope addressed from the school in the mailbox. When I got into the house, I placed it on the console table near the front door. I texted him.

You have some mail from the school. Want me to open it? I

texted him hoping he would've said I could.

Okay, and no, I'll open it when I get back.

I walked up one of our two staircases that led to the second floor of our mini mansion. I walked through our lengthy halls to our room over to my closet and then to my honey body wash stash. Marshall loved it when I wore that fragrance. I always wore it when Marshall went out and acted a fool. It was his favorite and I would get him back in my arms whenever he smelled it. That night was the night I was going to get my husband back.

I wore my royal blue sequin mermaid fishtail gown that draped to the floor. The back crisscrossed with rhinestone and laid lightly on my back. It was fitting, laid on every curve on my body, and let me not forget it gripped my ass just right. The color of the dress brought out my eyes. I put on my diamond watch, necklace, and earrings. I had to look fine, fine. I had to be the talk of Graysville University. He always said I was his showoff piece. That's probably all I became to him. I finished off the outfit with the perfect shoe, my gold red bottoms.

I heard Marshall pulling in the driveway. He beeped twice. That was my cue to make my grand entrance and show him what he was missing.

"You've been dressed since you left earlier?" I said before letting myself into the car. "Oh, and thanks for opening the door," I said sarcastically.

I always tried to ignore signs, but chivalry was dead.

"Yes, got dressed here before I picked up the tickets, and my bad, I am just a little nervous."

"You must be really nervous," I muttered; my eyes wandered around to see if I could spot anything out of the ordinary. There was an open duffle bag on the floor of the backseat. Marshall had changed somewhere else. His bag packed with his white v neck, gray shorts, sneakers, and a bag with travel-size toiletries was a dead giveaway.

"Oh, Okay. Cool." I replied. I had to control my temperature. Couldn't let the bag out of its hat. Not until I knew who she was.

We arrived at his school, and I noticed he hadn't said anything about his favorite honey body wash. The nerve of me to try to look and smell like something.

"Soo, you never said how I looked."

"You straight. You look decent, but maybe you should start wearing a different perfume. That one is kind of wack."

The nerve. His girl had his head all the way fucked up. That bitch was good.

We got to his school and they had beautiful LED colorful rotating lights that gave off a luxurious ambiance. Felt like we were entering into Hollywood. The traffic directors with welcome printed big on the front of their shirts guided us into the parking lot. A big school banner hung on the front of the building. The only thing on my mind was to find that bimbo that had my husband tied under her little finger.

We walked through the door, and I noticed big blown-up pictures of different students on the wall; the header read who moved the most drugs this year. That was pharmacy lingo, I guess. Before I could start my investigation, it seemed like a million people bummed rushed us. "Hey Marshall," everyone said in unison and it echoed throughout the crowd.

"Hey, everybody. I would like you to meet one of the closest people in my life." He introduced me like I was his damn mom.

Really? "Hey, everyone, nice to meet you all."

They greeted me with extended arms. I took a step back, dodging their hugs.

"I am his wife. Nice to meet you."

They stepped back and waved at me. "Hi, it's nice to meet you too."

I whispered to Marshall through my tightened lips and brushed my shoulder against his, "But who knew I was your wife seeing you don't have on your wedding ring."

He was really feeling ole girl, huh? He didn't even bother to wear his ring. Not even around me, his wife.

"Where is your ring?" I turned to him immediately after his friends walked away.

"Oh, shoot. I must have left it at the house. It was hurting my finger. "See?" He pointed at his ring finger. "It left a bruise." There was a deep imprint from the ring and a few marks.

"Yeah, you probably tried to pull yo whole damn finger off trying to take it off and hide it, but, I guess I see what you are talking about."

He spotted some friends from across the room.

"Huh?" he asked, his eyes blinked rapidly in discomfort.

"Nothing." I shook my head.

He shook his head like he was shaking some sense into it." But, baby. Let me say hi to some friends. I'll meet you back right here. Do you want a plate of food or a drink?"

"Yes, I want both, and I'll try not to get too drunk because you know how I'll get. Ronnie will turn into someone else." I smirked.

"Yeah, I know. But, take it easy tonight. I'll bring your stuff right over."

I ate and walked around. I looked for any information about Marshall's side piece. I looked through picture books and photos on the wall. I came across a list of top pharmacists, and I knew I wasn't going to see any pictures of my husband being a scholar. He hasn't been smart for a while. Especially thinking he is going to get away with cheating on me again.

After drinking a couple of drinks, I got so bored, and we had only been there for an hour and a half. I was ready to go. My mind was blown because I couldn't find shit about this girl. Plus, I didn't even know how the fuck she looked. I had to find a way to get out of there. I browsed through my phone to see who could come to pick me up.

I came across Coles's text, and I texted him back.

Hey, I know it's late, but are you available to go over the portfolio now?

Text tone.

Yes, sure. Where should we meet?

Well, I am at a reception right now. Can you pick me up from here?

Yes, but I am going to have to charge you. Lol, I'm just playin'.

Lol, I am glad you are playin'. Well, I am ready now. The address is 10156 S Lane street.

Okay, I'll be on my way in five mins.

Oh, yeah, can you act like my cab driver?

Yes, but can I ask why?

Because I just want to make a peaceful escape out of here.

Okay, whatever you say, Mrs. Valentine.

I walked around, looking for Marshall for about 15 minutes. When I finally found him, he was with a couple of guys.

I lightly tapped him on the shoulder. "I am getting tired and want to go home. I am also a bit tipsy and need to get some rest."

"But, we just got he—"

"She is fine." Someone yelled from the crowd right behind us.

Marshall smiled politely, but he wasn't too happy about that compliment from the way he bit his bottom lip. Marshall was overprotective.

"Oh, you don't have to leave. Stay here. I've already called a private driver," I informed him.

Text tone.

I'm outside.

"The driver just got here. He is waiting out front."

Marshall walked me to the car, but not before he yelled to his friends that he'd be back. "You sure you don't want me to take you home." He knew damn well he didn't want to take me home. He seemed very anxious to walk me to my ride.

"No, I'll be fine." I laid a kiss on his cheek. As mad as I was, I still wanted to love him.

"How are you doing?" Marshall asked Cole. "You sure you don't want me to take you home." He grabbed my hand and helped me into the truck.

"No, I am fine. I'll call you when I get home."

"Okay, make sure you get my wife home." Marshall made eye contact with Cole.

"I will," Cole said through his bright white smile.

"Alright, then baby. I'll see you when you get home. Enjoy yourself and congratulations."

Marshall closed the door and waved bye.

There was no reason for me to stay there. I couldn't find anything on Marshall's mystery woman, and he wanted to chit chat with his little friends. When we pulled off, I saw the girl from the yacht party again. She walked up the street with some guy with their arms interlocked.

I yelled and waved my hand out of the window. "Hey, Casey, girl. I didn't know you went here."

"Yes, girl. I am graduating this year, and I anxious to start a new life.

"I know that's right, but congratulations. Who is that with you, your boyfriend?

"Girl, my other brother."

"Well, I am heading out. Enjoy yourself."

Cole pulled off into traffic. I should've asked Casey if she knew Marshall. Cole turned up his music. He played a very relaxing instrumental with nature sounds. I felt like I was at a dental office for oral surgery. My body loosen, and I dozed off, but I heard everything that was going on around me.

"So, what was that...what was that all about?" he yelled over the music.

I lifted myself back in a sitting position. My body was slouched and leaned over the middle seat. I put my seat-belt on to hold me in place just in case I dozed off again.

"Are you okay back there?" he looked through the rear-view mirror to check on me.

"Yes, I am okay." I looked back at him through his rear-view mirror.

"Okay, so you are okay, but what was that all about back there? If you don't mind me asking." He cleared his throat.

"What was what about?" I asked.

"It seemed like you were trying to get out of there as soon as possible." He shifted his head from the mirror to pay attention to the road.

I continued to stare at him through the mirror. "I don't

know what you mean. I am just sleepy and had to go home. I didn't want to ruin his night, so I had to call someone to pick me up."

"Oh, why didn't you call Lori?"

"Wow, what's with all the questions? I called you. Was that a problem?"

"Yeah, I didn't mean it like that. You are fine. I mean, yes, that's fine with me, Mrs. Valentine."

"Ha-Ha-Ha...You know you play too much." If he only knew how much I needed that compliment and that laugh. "But enough about me. What were you doing when I called?"

"Nothing much. Watching television and working on some other work...hey," he yelled.

I dozed off again. "I am sorry I was listening."

"But anyway, it smells like honey in here. Is that some type of honey fragrance that you have on? If so, it smells great."

"Yes, that's all me. Glad you like." He had a good sense of smell because I thought I smelled more like alcohol.

"So, what's the address? I don't know where we are going."

"Oh, I'm sorry. Its 4336 N Maryseal Ave."

"That's not too far from where I live. I live in a village around the corner.

"Really?

"Yes."

"No wonder it didn't take you long to come to get me." We pulled up to the front of the gate of my village. Hayes buzzed us through. Cole pulled into my driveway. He got out, walked around, and opened his car door for me. He extended his hand for me to grab and helped me inside my house.

"Would you like something to drink? Some water, wine, champagne, or soda? I offered.

"Champagne?" He said wide-eyed.

"Yes, what's wrong with champagne?"

"Nothing. Are we having some kind of celebration or something?"

"No, we are not." I giggled. "Champagne is not just for celebrations. It's just like having wine, but better."

"If you say so, Mrs. Valentine. But I'll just take some water. If you don't mind?"

I walked him to the seating area right off the kitchen. The lounge sofa we had was so comfortable, but one wrong move it took you in like quicksand. We could see everything around us from that view. You could see the pool out back, our big yard, and into Gale's bedroom window. Cole pulled out the proposal from his black suitcase that I hadn't even seen him bring in. He handed it to me.

"As you can see, if you look through the folder, I've written up documents in full detail. You can also see—"

"Okay, this looks nice." The drinks that I had from the reception and that champagne I drank with Cole had me feeling myself. I didnt even want to talk about the proposal anymore. I wanted to dance, but I knew I had to keep it together. I had to show him I was a business-woman. I flipped to the next page in the proposal.

"So, you are telling me that if I put this amount of money into my business, I will triple in less than a year? Ha, sounds like a plan. How do you want to move forward?" I placed the folder down on my glass table. I thought about Marshall and all the shit I had been through with his ass. All his damn cheating and embarrassment. I've never cheated on him. I've always been loyal. Never looked at another man in any way. Men tried to seduce me every day. Marshall knew I was fine, but he didn't care.

"Hellooo?" Cole waved his hand in front of my face. "Are you there?"

I placed my champagne down on the table. I accidentally spilled my glass on the folder.

"OMG!" I reached to grab my throw cover from behind him to clean up the mess.

"It's okay. Maybe we should talk more about it another time. It seems that you have other things on your mind." Cole reached over to help me clean up.

CHAPTER 5

It's Fair Game

I looked up, and our lips connected, and I wasn't mad about it. I kissed him, and he kissed me back. He had been waiting from the jump, and I made his dream come true.

His lips were so tender, and when our tongues connected, the energy that our bodies were sharing had my body feeling as if it was on fire. That was the most satisfying kiss I've had in a while.

I could see the inside of my eyelids, and when I opened them, I saw the outside of his. I grabbed his hand and placed it inside my dress onto my breast. My pussy screamed his name. He pushed me onto the arm of the couch and squeezed my breast. My body felt faint when he sucked down the neck past my collarbone onto my firm nipples. His lips demanded me. He started to taste them and caressed me.

"How does that feel?" he asked.

I grabbed his biceps, and my toes curled. I couldn't answer him. He knew exactly what he was doing. He leaned on my body more and gripped my thighs. He moved my panties to the side and felt his way up my pussy with his finger. I moaned. It was off guard, but it was well needed. He stroked his finger in and out of me while savoring my breast. He licked and sucked on both my bare breast using a tongue motion that I imagined he would do to my clit. I climaxed. My pussy just told him how it felt. He took his finger out of me, and it dripped with my juices. I climbed on top of him, and he ripped the rest of my dress off. That was the moment I knew he'd been waiting for.

The glitter from my dress surrounded his mouth. We began to kiss while I unbuttoned his pants. His dick was thick and hard when I gripped and pulled it out. I grabbed his dick to put his it inside of me, he pulled out a gold wrapper. "Protection is key." He bit his bottom lip. I put the condom on his dick with my mouth. The head touched the hanging thing in the back of my throat; I didn't gag.

He pulled me up to him. His big warm curved upward dick called for my G-spot, and that's when I straddled his lap. I gripped his thick lethal object and introduced it to my inner parts. My pussy gripped his throbbing dick.

Wham.Wham.Wham. I bounced up and down on his monster. My ass cheeks smacked his thighs. He palmed my ass cheeks, picked me up, and walked over to the window. He pressed me against the window while maintaining a steady rhythm. He sucked on my neck while I moaned and grunted. He felt so amazing inside of me. He bounced me up and down and gripped my ass that he plastered against my floor to ceiling window. It was so hot that the windows steamed up and made my ass and back moist.

He took me over to the table in the corner and bent me over. I glanced out of the window, and I saw Gale looking at me through her bedroom window. She smiled and waved. She probably saw the pleasure in my doggy style position. It was so embarrassing, but it felt so good. He put his dick further in me while palming my ass. My jaw dropped and I howled. It sounded like an effect out of a movie. We climaxed. He kissed me across my ass cheeks and straight up my back. He turned me around and kissed me down to my stomach. I looked back through the window. Gale was gone. He walked off. His back and ass were muscular and tight. OMG! This man got me feeling some type of way.

My phone rang and lit up on the kitchen island.

I ran over to answer.

I knew it was Marshall checking in. "Hello?"

He sounded intoxicated. "Why didn't you call me when you got in?"

"I am sorry I got home about fifteen mins from the time I left you." Damn, I've only been home for an hour and a half. "But I am okay. Sorry for not calling. I am very sleepy."

"Why does it sound like you are out of breath?" Sweat dripped down my phone onto my forearm.

"I am not out of breath. The phone scared me when it rang. Just a little startled, that's all. I have to turn the volume down on my phone. The ring, yeah, it was just the ring. It shocked me." My voice crackled.

"Well, okay. Get some rest. I am going to stay at my friend's house tonight. I am not in any condition to drive right now." Music blasted in his background; a girl's voice sounded like she was right next to him.

"Okay, that's fine. I'll see you in the morning. Don't forget; you are married."

I should have taken my own advice.

"What's that supposed to mean?" his voice sounded much clearer.

I looked at Cole. He was sitting down, gulping down the rest of his water. "Nothing. Goodnight. See you tomorrow."

Click.

I grabbed some paper towels and wiped down the sweat from my phone.

I walked toward Cole, who was sitting on the couch, studying my physique. "It's kind of late and you shouldn't be driving after having a major climax like that, ha ha".

Cole laughed as if I was one of his favorite comedians.

"Would you like to stay the night?" I walked toward the couch and placed the rest of the paper towels on the table where we were sitting. My foot got caught behind the other. I stumbled a little before I found my balance.

"Don't fall. That's a lot of sweat." He jumped up to run to my rescue. "With all this sweat, I know I don't need to go to the gym tomorrow," he said.

I grabbed a towel to wipe myself down.

"You funny, but yeah, I can stay to make sure you have a great rest of the night." He grabbed his dick that sat on his thigh.

We walked upstairs with not one piece of clothing on our asses. We laid in the bed facing the ceiling. Our bodies touched, and I got so turned on by Cole's cologne and sweat. I rolled over to my side and placed my leg across his. He stretched his right arm out, and I laid my head on his biceps. Maybe I shouldn't have done what I did next, but the temptation called me. I gripped his dick, rotating my fingers massaging it. I rubbed my rotating fingers down his penis and then up to his hard tip. I motioned my thumb around the crease of his head. I wanted to stop, but the way he bit his lips kept me going. He grunted, he ejaculated, and his slime streamed down my hand.

He looked over at me. The look of satisfaction and his big bright smile let me know that I had snatched his soul right out of him. "It's like that, Mrs. Valentine." He stared at me while I walked to the shower. The next thing I knew, he got out of the bed and followed me.

When I woke up for work, I turned around to see if Cole was still there. Marshall laid next to me instead. I leaned over to give him an enormous kiss, but I hesitated because he had a lipstick stain already placed there. "Oh, you were out with your bitch last night, huh?" I shoved him. He woke up disoriented. He caught himself before he fell out of bed onto the floor. "You were out with your bitch last night, huh?"

His eyes darted back and forth. "What are you talking about? I was with the guys last night."

"Oh, so the guys wear lipstick. You must think I am a goofy, huh? Make sure you clean up next time. You smell like perfume and booze. Dude, you are wrong for that." I yanked the covers off me and threw them on him. On my way to the restroom, I glanced over at the clock on the nightstand. On the floor under the nightstand was an open condom. I bent over to pick it up quickly. "And kiss my ass," I said to him while I slowly gripped the condom.

After I raced to the bathroom, I turned on the shower and flushed the condom down the toilet. Where the hell did Cole go? I hoped his ass was not hiding under the bed. What if he was on the balcony? I would be fucked.

Can we meet again soon to go over the portfolio? I texted him.

Text tone

Yes, we can.

Okay. What's a good time? Where are you right now?

Oh, I'll let you know by the end of the day. I am on my way to work.

OMG! That was close, but that was so fun. I grabbed a

towel from the back of the door and wiped the sweat and anxiousness from my face.

On my way to work, I was more furious than ever. I didn't know if I was madder because he was with ole girl or because I almost got caught. I was not good at the whole cheating thing. It was my first, and I hoped it was my last. A girl who never cheats, cheats in her own damn home. Damn, that was a good ass slogan for a shirt.

I pulled up to my job, and my mind couldn't handle everything I was thinking. I knew I couldn't focus when I almost ran a stop sign, hit a person and their dog, and jumped a curb. One thing was clear; I needed to be more careful before I killed myself or ended up in jail. I walked through the door at my job. I hadn't seen that place in so long, and in due time, I planned not to be there at all. I walked to my desk and happy nobody said anything slick to me about me taking my paid time off because I would have most likely cussed their asses out. On my way to my desk, I looked down at my phone and I tried not to make eye contact with anyone. I bumped into one of my co-workers.

"Hey, how have you been? We missed you. You want coffee or a doughnut, where have you been?" He talked very fast like he was on drugs or something. He always blew me with that. Like, take a breather sometimes.

At the end of the day, those people were so damn nosy that you couldn't blink without them wanting to know why. I took off for three days WITH an early notice, and he acts as if I've vacationed for a month.

"Oh, I've been good. Just enjoying and celebrating with my husband." If only I could tell him how much of a bastard my husband was, I would've. "But, I'll have to talk to you later. I have to catch up on so much work."

"Okay, well, maybe I'll introduce you to our new co-worker later."

"May-be, but I'll see you later. Bye."

"Alright then." He stood right in the doorway that led to the hallway to my office.

"Take care Alex and have a great rest of the day," I said with a smile so large it couldn't be authentic. My cheeks started to hurt from that fake ass smile I gave him. He finally got the memo after we stood in front of each other with nothing more to say.

"Ohhh, I'm sorry." He stepped to the side, and I maneuvered around him.

I fucked, fucked Cole the night before, and Marshall fucked, fucked that girl last night. Although I stepped out of our marriage, I still could be mad; this is my first fuck to his twenty thousandth fuck. Even though I wanted to tear the office apart because of built up anger, it felt good to be one of the bad guys. I stopped in the breakroom to grab some coffee on my way to my desk. On my way out the door, I grabbed another one. I didn't want to have to go back and have to talk to anyone else.

When I got to my desk, I started to think about Cole. I dialed him and before he picked up, I hung up because I had nothing to say. Instead, I tracked Marshall's phone. He was now at an unfamiliar address. I wondered if that was his girl's place.

I packed up to raise hell, but I had so much work to do, and I couldn't let him fuck up my money.

I finished early and tracked his phone again. He had the nerve to be there still. I followed the tracking app to the address where he was. When I got there, his car was parked out front. While sitting there, a homeless man walked past, and I whistled for him to come over to my car. I asked him if he could put a note on Marshall's car window. I wrote the word bitch in large capital letters. At first, I was going to ask him to leave it on the bitches' condo window, but that would've been too risky. He'd still get the point.

Before I pulled off, I thought about going up there and fucking some shit up, but my bowels were moving like crazy. I should've never drunk all that damn coffee. That's what I get for being greedy and shit. For some insane reason, I started to think about Cole again. I would've called him, but I didn't know what to say. I did know one thing, though; I knew where Marshall's girl lived, and I would have to do another drive by once I got my bowels under control.

When Marshall got home, I acted as if nothing had ever happened. I started cooking, but it ate me alive to know that he was cheating on me again, and I knew where his bitch lived now.

"Did you go back to your chick house the other night," I giggled, aggressively.

"What are you talking about?" His eyes darted from side to side.

"Earlier today, you weren't here. So, where were you?'

"I was at the school. I had to pick up my graduation tickets."

He must've thought I was the dumbest bitch alive. Maybe because I always acted like it. My naïve ways tried to keep our relationship/marriage together. "Right, so that happened. Did you get them? Where are they?"

He walked away. "I don't have time for this shit, Ronnie."

"Like I thought you didn't go get no damn tickets."

Phone rang.

Hello?

"Hey, It's Cole.

My heart damn near stopped. That's what I get for not looking at the number before I picked up.

"Oh, Hey." I whispered.

"Would you like to meet up again to really talk about business?"

"Yes, when are you free."

"Now," Cole replied.

"Meet you at your office in 15 minutes. Send me the address."

When I walked up to Cole's office, I could see him looking at me like he wanted to have me for breakfast, lunch, and dinner. I was too busy focusing on my career and Marshall breaking my heart every other year to find someone else to love, but I became fed up. When the doors closed, I grabbed the back of his neck and kissed him. This kiss was more passionate than the first. The only other kiss I've had besides Marshall was a kiss on the cheek from my mother and my mother in law with her crusty lip ass. He grabbed me, threw me on his desk. He pulled up my pencil skirt. "Do you want me?" He rolled his long thick tongue like a water wave.

I nodded my head, and I gripped the edge of his desk for dear life. He hooked his hands on my thigh; he made sure I took all of his tongue in me. I couldn't take it anymore. I didn't know how he knew, but before I climaxed, he pulled his fingers in and out of me for the finish.

After a successful meeting, Cole walked me back to the car, and we kissed again. After that night, I saw him two or three more times that week. It was risky meeting him at his office so late, but who gave a damn. He had marketed himself so well that I wanted him more and more.

As much as I tried to stay away from him, it just didn't happen. So yes, I saw Cole more than I should have. I told Marshall I was with Maxine and Maxine that was getting a bazillion wax. I told Lori I was with my mom and my mom that I was with Lori. Yeah, I didn't give a fuck if anybody found out. I just tried to keep everyone busy.

It made me feel so good to be valued again. I didn't care if it's just lust. Cole put me first, and he didn't have to. It's not like I was his girl or anything. I hadn't even ask Cole if he had a girlfriend, wife, ex-wife, or close friend. I didn't even know if he had any close relatives, how old he was, his last name, and whether he had any kids. I didn't know shit, but I did know dick was bomb thoooo. I didn't want to think about it too much. I just wanted to have fun.

I am a valued woman.

CHAPTER 6

Graduation Day

One Week Later

I pulled up to the graduation in my emerald green BMW. I was not going to lie; I had outdone myself. My sunglasses by themselves said that I was a bad bitch. My glasses were working double duty. Not only did they keep me fly, but I hid behind them. I couldn't let anybody see my eyes wander around. I was my own private investigator, and I had to see if his girl was there. The graduation was also outside, so that was also great to my advantage.

While I scanned the lawn, I locked eyes with my mother in law. I knew she would take a lot of time out of my investigation, but I walked over to greet both her and my father in law. "How have you been, Ronnie?" My mother in law smiled. She wore an orange midi dress that matched her sun hat. She paired it with a silver metallic belt that matched her shoes and purse.

"I've been pretty good." I lied. I had been pretty good at lying lately.

"This is such an exciting day for us all. All your hard work and dedication to our son is about to pay off, Ronnie." She congratulated me as if I were graduating with him. We walked to our seats.

"It sure is. I am so proud of Marshall." Fuck that bitch and I don't care if he had been working hard. "His graduation is all he's been talking about for the last couple of weeks." We made it to our row of seats. We sat five rows back from the announcer. "Well, here are our seats. I am going to go to the little girl's room before the ceremony starts." My mother in law was a big distraction with all her small talk. She really thought that I was there for a ceremony. She better had hoped it wouldn't be a funeral ceremony happening by the end of that week.

I noticed the line was pretty long in the bathroom. I skimmed the line looking for Marshall's side piece. I prayed for a sign. I didn't see ole girl, but I did see Casey standing at the very front. She was lucky to have that spot. "Hey, girl," I yelled. A couple of girls turned around, but Casey didn't hear me. "Hey, girl," I repeated.

I caught her attention, when she finally turned around we locked eyes. "Oh, heyyyy. We keep running into each other," She said vigorously.

"I know, right. what are you doing here?" I yelled back to her.

"I'm sorry for being so loud in your ear." I apologized to the lady in front of me.

"Hey girl, I graduate today." She spun around, strutted, and then vogued.

"What are you here for?" she fixed her hair. The spinning almost knocked her curl pattern loose.

"Oh yeah, I'm sorry, I forgot, and my husband graduates today too." I smiled, forcefully. She was the last thing on my mind.

"Oh, okay. I want to meet your husband. You can meet my boyfriend too." She walked in the bathroom stale.

"Okay, girl. I'll try to catch up with you after the ceremony." The line stopped moving, and more people were coming in.

I needed less time in the bathroom and more time outside. When I walked from behind the restrooms swinging door, there were eyes all on me like I just committed a crime. I knew I looked good, but damn. I scanned the crowd and I still didn't see that trick. I imagined his side piece would have on a big ass jogging suit again and she might've been hiding because she knew who I was. I walked back over to my seat; Marshall stood by his lame friends over by the stage. He wore his Alma Marta school colors; a dark blue straight legged suit with a red tie and white button-up shirt. When he saw me, he turned his head. I guessed the clown was still mad about whatever the fuck he was mad about. He was going to be even more upset once I found out who his little trick was.

The ceremony started, and they called the last names in alphabetical order. It was a while before they got to Marshall's name. I looked around, and there was still no sight of his girl. I mean, how the hell would I know who she was? I've only seen her in that damn jogging suit. I thought once they called his name, I would spot her cheering. That would give me a chance to look around the crowd and see who is shouting his name the loudest. I was sure there would be hundreds of hoochies on their feet, but I was sure it would be someone who would do the very most.

As soon as they got to the graduates whose last name began with the letter V, I was all eyes and ears.

"Marshall Valentine," the announcer said over the microphone.

My eyes scanned the lawn very quickly and observed every hoochies movement. But there were far too many hoochies that screamed, jumped, and danced. You would've thought we were at a concert. Like Marshall was a fucking celebrity. I sat down and gathered my thoughts. Maybe she wasn't there because he knew I would be there. Maybe he respected me enough to know not to bring anyone in my space. He must've loved me after all.

As the ceremony was coming to a close, people gathered around to wait for their graduates to take pictures. I made reservations a while back for Marshall's graduation dinner, and although I still didn't want to celebrate with him, a bish was hungry. I browsed the crowd looking for Marshall, and I spotted him talking to Casey. I guessed they did know each other.

I walked over, and Casey smiled at me. She turned Marshall around to face me.

"Hey, girl. I want you to meet m—"

"Oh, I see you already met m—"

"Boy-friend," she revealed

"Hus-ba—" I hesitated.

A ball of fire ran down my shoulder to my arm and then to my fist. I swung toward Marshall. "Why me?" I yelled.

I jumped in his direction. I swung again and it flew past his face.

How could he do this to me? My reaction was if I didn't know he had been cheating. But he had the person standing right in my face, and I knew of her. It looked like a setup.

"Why have me come to a graduation that you knew your side chick would be at? Nah, fuck that, who would be graduating with you?"

WHAM. WHAM.

My fist connected twice to his jaw.

Marshall's head flew, and his cheek hit his right shoulder. He slightly stumbled. At that moment I wish I had Mike Tysons strength and knocked his ass out. Casey jumped at me, and I smacked her ass in the face. My hand was in so much pain, but the pain didnt stop that ass whooping from happening. Marshall was holding his face with one hand and Casey with the other. I managed to jumped on his back and wrapped my arms across his neck.

Small gasps escaped his throat, "Ronnie, you... are... choking me." He tried to peel my arms from his neck.

"That's the point, dumbass."

Bystanders ran from each side of the lawn to see what was going on. Some grabbed me while I kicked him all in the crack of his ass.

"You thought I didn't know. Dumbass, I knew you had a bitch on the side, and Casey, I am going to break yo fuckin' face if I get to you." I grabbed and pushed people trying to get through the crowd. "So ya'll were working together or some shit?! Marshall, did you know that I met this bitch before?" I jumped up, extended my leg to kick Casey.

"Ronnie, calm down," Marshall yelled.

"Calm down?!" I grabbed the nearest graduation cap off someone's head and threw it at Marshall so hard it popped him in the frontal part of his head. I tried to crack his fucking skull.

Marshall massaged the spot where the corner on the hat hit him. "Damn, Ronnie. Stop," he yelled. I sneakily walked toward Casey. I grabbed the curls in her hair.

Two hands grabbed my arms from behind. I turned to see who it was, and it was Maxine. She tried to pull me back. I shifted side to side, trying to break Maxine's grip.

"Let her go, bitch!" a very familiar and surprising voice said from over my shoulder. Lori came through the crowd out of nowhere with her arm extended in front of her, palms opened, and pushed Maxine off me. I ran toward Marshall, but before I could get a chance to kick him in the nuts, the security guards grabbed Lori and me. They peeled my fingers out of what was left of Casey's curled hair. While they focused on me letting go of Casey, I quickly moved closer to Marshall and kicked his ass in the dick. I tried to crush all his shit up while still holding Casey's hair. "Bitch," I yelled at him.

"Stop it, Ronnie." Marshall's mom screamed.

"Maxine, you knew, huh?" I looked toward her in disgust.

She stood closer to Marshall. "No, I didn't, Ronnie, I promise I didn't," she pleaded.

"Don't let me catch you later, Maxine. You slick ass bitch," Lori yelled.

Lori and I walked off scott-free. The security guards agreed to let us go if we complied with them to leave and don't come back.

We agreed and made it back to my car. "Lori, what are you doing here?"

"Shiiit, I came to beat someone's ass, obviously," She laughed, balled her fist up, and jumped back and forth like she was in a boxing ring.

"No, like for real. How did you know where I was?"

"Oh, I tracked your phone."

"You tracked my phone?" I stared at her over the hood of the car before we got in.

"Bish yes, I tracked your got damn phone. You were acting all strange and keeping secrets. You didn't look like yourself. I came to see if you were okay. I had a feeling, that's all."

I jumped over the armrest to hug her. "I love you bitch!" I kissed her on the cheek.

"I love you too bitch, and that's what cousins are fooooorrrrr," she sang.

"Ugh, girl no. Don't sing, but, wait, where is your car?"

"Oh, I called a private driver. Girl, I told you I had a feeling," we laughed.

"So, what the hell happened back there?"

"Well, remember back at the coffee shop when I pulled Maxine to the side?" She nodded her head. "Well, I asked her if she knew if Marshall was cheating on –"

She yelled, "I knew it. I knew it. You were, looking too weird, girl. I knew you were hiding somethin'. Why couldn't you just tell me what was going on?"

"Because knowing you, Lori. I wouldn't even have known who the girl was. You would have confronted him, and he probably would've told the bitch he had to stop talking to her, and I would not have gotten this far."

"True. True. You know me too well. I don't play. I'd fight a bitch. Period. Where do you want to go?'

"I am taking you home, and then I am going home and no, I don't need you to stay with me. I'll be okay. I am already knowin' you want to fuck Marshall up, but no, I got this."

Marshall had the nerve to bring his punk ass home that night. He walked through the door with flowers. I couldn't believe it, it seemed to be one big joke to him. His tie had been untied, and he had specks of blood on his white button-up. He looked exhausted.

"I'm sorry. I'm so sorry. Forgive me," he begged.

"Boy, Don't try to give me those got damn flowers you got for your graduation. Are you stupid?" I stood up from our sofa and walked over to him.

"These aren't from my graduation. I got these for you."

"Oh and you didn't call me to see if I was okay, but I bet you made sure that bitch was okay."

He stood there and looked brainless.

"Ain't no damn sorry. You got the nerve to walk in the house at this time of night with some damn flowers." I reached to grab the flowers from him with a smile. I smacked him across his face with them. "Get yo dumb ass out of here with that shit. Where the fuck you know, a 24-hour flower shop? I told you the other day. Stop thinking I am a goofy. It's going to get you fucked up. You saw the way I did your girl."

He continued to look brainless and bug-eyed.

"You know what."

He walked toward me. He looked so stressed. He opened and closed his mouth a dozen times like he was struggling with what to say next.

I stepped back. "And you know what. I knew who that bitch was for forever. Do you want to know how we knew each other? We met at the yacht party when I was with Maxine."

"How the hell was I supposed to know that, Ronnie?"

"Was that a rhetorical question? Are you serious? You didn't have to know. If you weren't out there cheating, there wouldn't be a reason to know."

He extended his arms for a hug.

I pushed them to the side.

He waved his hand dismissively and walked away.

"You feel dumb yet?" I yelled.

I sat back on the sofa and texted Cole. I explained to him what happened and that I needed him to come get me. I laid on the couch, curled up, and waited on a response. Marshall walked back in. He sat on the side of me and tried to explain everything that happened. It was too late. I didn't even care anymore.

"You should've told me this a long time ago. I don't want to hear that shit right n—"

I frowned at the sound of the doorbell. We looked at each other.

"It better not be your girl." I threatened.

He smacked his lips.

Knock. Knock. Knock.

"Marshall, go and answer the damn door. It's probably your bitch coming to check on you to see if you got your ass whooped some more," I asserted. He hadn't moved an inch. Maybe he knew I was right. "Why are you still sitting here? Go check it out." I shoved him.

He placed both hands on the couch and pushed himself up. He walked over to the door at a slow pace showing he feared whatever was on the other side of the door. He peeked through the peephole, and my body amped up. Although I was beat and wanted to rest, I prepared myself to knock a bitch out, on sight.

Bang.Bang.Bang.

The door shook and the hinges rattled.

"Whoever it is, is angry," I yelled from the sofa. I hoped it was Casey. No one would have been able to stop us.

"It's the police," the voice on the other side of the door yelled. "Open the door now."

"What's the problem officer," Marshall's voice crackled.

"I am only going to say this once more. Open the door

before I open it for you," the officer's voice got more aggressive.

Marshall opened the door slowly.

"Is anyone else in here?" the officer asked.

"Yes, sir. My wife." Marshall looked as if he was going to pee his pants.

"Would her name be Ronnie Lawson?"

"Yes, that's her," Marshall replied.

"Ronnie," he yelled. "The police want to talk to you."

The palms of my hands sweated, my heart pounded in my ears, and I couldn't move, I couldn't lift a finger. I felt paralyzed. The police? I've only had a few run-ins with the police, and it was nothing too serious. It was just for a few speeding tickets. What did this police officer want with me? If that bitch pressed charges. Marshall was going to feel my wrath.

"Ronnie," he repeated. He was so scared he didn't even ask what the officer needed me for. He just sold me out.

I inhaled deeply and then exhaled. I started to feel some circulation in my legs. I strolled over to the corner of the wall and peeked around. The officer faced the opposite way looking up, over, and around waiting for me to come out. He turned in my direction, and I couldn't believe who was standing there. It was Cole, and oh my, he looked so good. My state of mind changed, and a weight lifted off my shoulders. My body got so warm; my body symbolized my girl downstairs. I cannot believe how he just made it happen after only one text message. Yeah, I knew for sure I would fuck him that night.

I sashayed my way over to the door where they stood. "How can I help you, officer?" I said hesitant but flirtatious.

"I got a complaint from someone at Graysville Uni-

versity that you were in an altercation at today's graduation," he said with his hand on his belt pulling his pants
up above his tucked-in shirt. He stood there dressed from
head to toe in police uniform. The visor part of his hat
covered most of his face.

"Oh, so your bitch called the police, huh?" I said to Marshall but stared at Cole's perfectly fitted uniform. "And
how do I know that you are an officer," I asked Cole.

Cole pulled a badge out of his perfectly creased pants
pocket and flashed it at us swiftly. When he put the badge
in his pocket, I followed his hand, and my eyes locked on
his monster print.

"Nah, she wouldn't do that." Marshall looked down at
me to confirm.

I gave him a look of disappointment. If looks could
kill, he would've been dead.

He leaned back on the broad door frame with and gave
me a weak ass puppy dog face. The face a dog gives when
you tell them to stop acting up and they get in trouble
because they can't.

"How the fuck do you know?!" I badgered, not looking
at him anymore.

"Look, I don't have time for this. You must come down
to the station," Cole ordered.

"Officer, it's seven at night. Could she come in the
morning?" Marshall complained

"If she were able to come to the station in the morning,
I wouldn't be here right now, now would I?"

That's right check his punk ass, Officer Cole.

"She better hope that she gets out in the morning," he
said to Marshall.

Marshall shook his head up and down and looked off to
the direction of our neighbor's house.

"Well, officer, I guess we have to go to the station for some questioning." I bit and sucked at my bottom lip, looking at Cole. My mouth was moist and ready for a him. Marshall was so busy staring off into space with a striking vacant look on his face that he didn't catch on to the flirting Cole and I were doing.

"Babe, I am sorry." He grabbed my hand and pleaded. "Can I come with her to the station?" He turned toward Cole.

"There is no point. There is nothing that you can do." He assured Marshall. "Now, Ronnie Lawson come with me." He grabbed me by my arm with his soft muscular hands.

He wrapped his soft, warm hand around my waist, and we walked over to his car. Coles' car was not visible. He parked his vehicle behind my car, which hid on the side of Marshall. He put me in the backseat. Marshall wouldn't catch on if I paid him to. He didn't even make sure I was in the car before he ran back into the house. Marshall was so 'smart'.

We drove off, and he put the police siren on. We started to laugh hysterically. Cole worked fast, and that's what I liked about him. He saved me from continuing to get lied to. All the issues that Marshall and I had were the furthest from my mind.

"So, where in the hell did you get these sirens?"

"I borrowed them from a friend. That's why it took me a while to get to you," he chuckled.

"I like your uniform, Mr. Officer." I'm in love with a stripper by T-Pain played in my head.

Pressure started to build up in my girl downstairs. My pussy began to palpitate like a heartbeat. The throb became more intense and tighter as he continued to drive.

His uniform plus his cologne was a sure thing that my pussy was going to get pounded that evening. I looked at him through his rear-view mirror. My pussy was past moist, and my nipples were taut. I raised my shirt up and over my head. It fell on the seat next to me. I played with my nipples.

He glanced in the mirror back at me. "What are you doing, Miss. Lawson."

"Pull over to the side of the road right now." He didn't ask why, he knew what time it was. I continued to take my clothes off.

"Now bring yo fine ass back here and fuck me," I ordered.

He got out of the car and jumped in the back with me. I grabbed his dick, and it was so hard it could've crushed a brick of gold. It was time for a different kind of ride. He started to suck on my erect nipples. He nibbled then sucked while palming my left breast. I got on top of him and seized his dick. Dick was so big I had to use both hands. It felt much bigger than before. Maybe because I wasnt tipsy off champagne that time. But, from that day on, I called it my Black Anaconda. He inserted his middle finger in and out of pussy he then thrust it in and out of his mouth. I then introduced his anaconda to my tropical rainforest.

"Oooooooooooh, ooooooooh, oooooooohhhh-eee," he howled out. "Damn, yo shit stays wet," he complimented.

It's been over a week since I felt his anaconda in me. From the way he sat back and let me perform, let me know he had been waiting on my call. I had never given him all my tricks all at once, and that evening I decided to continue to only provide him with just a taste. I started to twerk up and down on his anaconda. I rode down onto my knees then back up to the tip of his length. When I got to the top of his thick tip he mumbled.

"You... like this... di-ck." He tried his best to say without losing focus and bustin' one.

"I love it," I replied. I clenched my teeth, taking all of Coles anaconda in me. I turned around with my back facing him and rode it from the rear. He palmed my ass cheeks and motioned for me to ride up and down, deeper and he penetrated me. His big hard dick made me want more and more. He grabbed my titties while I bounced up and down. After a couple of minutes into the ride, he laid me down and took me halfway to heaven. He spread my legs apart and flicked the tip of his tongue on my clit, and tongue kissed my vagina opening. I rubbed my hand across my uncovered nipples and up the side of my neck. I grabbed my breast, stroked them, caressed them, and I pulled on them. He put his tongue inside of me and rotated in circles. He licked my clit again, and I climaxed. "It... tastes... so... good," he said while his tongue played with my clit while I dripped. He put his dick back in and went to work. He pulled out and slime leaked on my stomach.

"So, what do you want to do now? I was thinking we should grab something to eat," he said as he wiped his mouth, me and himself with napkins that he got from the back pockets of the seat.

"Ayeee, yes, something to eat," I said, clowning. "But you just ate." I joked.

"So you think you're funny, huh?" He laughed loudly. "That was my appetizer. Now I need dinner and then later have you again for dessert."

"Oh really." I sat up and laid my legs across his legs.

"We can go to Grand Ru. I heard they are pretty good,"

he suggested.

"Yes, we can go there. I've never been there before."

Grand Ru was a very expensive restaurant. Much more lavish than that restaurant Marshall took his girl too. I couldn't believe he suggested to take me there. People usually go there to impress someone, first date, anniversary, so on and so forth. "Do you like me, Cole?" I said playfully. Even though I said it playfully, I really wanted to know.

"You straight," he said that like I wasn't shit. "Ha.Ha.Ha, just playing. I mean, what's not to like?" We started to put our clothes on and got situated in the front seat.

We smelled like all types of sex. I kind of liked it, but I had to make sure I got cleaned up before I returned home.

He started the car and we were on our way to the restaurant. "I hope no one is in this restaurant knows Marshall because I am supposed to be in jail. Ha-ha-ha."

"I am sure no one will see us where we will be seated, and before you ask, I am not a regular. Plugged life."

"Uh oh, in that case, take me back home. I don't need any more problems tonight, Mr. Officer, ha.ha."

Cole turned up the music, and we danced and sung all the way to the restaurant.

We pulled up. Cole ran around to my side of the car to open my door. The restaurant was beau-ti-ful. I had driven past it several times, but I'd never been that close. I wasn't no broke bitch tho. I wanted to save every dime I had for my firm. The front of the tall tan building was lit up. It looked like a palace with the red-carpet draping down the stairs. There were beautiful white hydrangea lined up along the stairs. Through the tall full glass windows and doors, you could see the enormous, beautiful chandeliers, and people looked their best. It was big fancy, fancy.

"How do you like it?" He asked like I was some ratchet chick that he brought out the hood for a little fun.

"It's nice. Like I imagined."

I was glad I still had on my fly ass outfit I wore to the graduation. Although it got a bit wrinkled from sex, I didn't feel underdressed. That restaurant was for people with money, with no exceptions. Cole was a PR agent plus more so yeah, he could afford it, but why would he take me here knowing what kind of relationship we've created. I am sure I was nothing more than a fuck to him.

We got to the door, and the greeter approached us. "Hey, Mr. Williams, are you here for two."

"Yes, that's right." He smiled, dominantly.

"How does he know you? If this isn't your usual."

Could I be just some other girl he does this with?

"Don't worry about that. Let's just enjoy ourselves," Cole insisted.

About thirty minutes later, the waitress came and got us and walked us to the back to a beautiful deck. The lights were beautifully lit. So bright and breathtaking. The breeze was just right. It was unbelievable. I had a complete blast before we even gotten started. The waitress grabbed my napkin and attempted to place it across my legs. "Rick, wait, I got that." Cole jumped up, grabbed the napkin, and laid it across my lap. "You had a long day. Let me cater to you."

It took everything in me not to jump over our table and give him some more of what we had done in the car. "This is beautiful. Thank you, Cole."

"No, problem beautiful." He grinned.

Our server came to the table. "Hey, Cole. I haven't seen

you on the back deck in a while. She must be special."

"She's A'ight, but next time let's keep that between you and me." He pointed his finger back and forth at him and the server.

"Oh, I'm so sorry, Cole. It will never happen again," he assured.

"It's okay. I still love ya," Cole laughed.

"Well then, are you guys ready to order."

"I am," I said. "I'd like the shrimp and lobster tails with extra butter. Side of mashed potatoes and butter rolls and whatever else comes with that. Also, can I please have a big glass of cold water?"

"Cool, give me my regular." Cole ordered.

We laughed, we flirted, and we kissed. The night was going so well that I forgot about everything that happened earlier that day. Marshall could have that bitch though. I didn't care if he wanted her or not; that was not my problem anymore. Being on that small and last-minute date with Cole showed me that there were men out there to treat me right. That man may not have been Cole, but I knew there was someone other than Marshall, thanks to Cole for the wakeup call. My communication with Cole was far from anything Marshall and I had ever had.

We pulled up to Coles' place. It looked just as beautiful as the Grand Ru without the people. I had no idea that there were mini mansions on the other side of the village where Marshall and I lived. I couldn't believe my eyes. I thought my house looked like something, but Cole's house stretched from corner to corner. His gorgeous, extensive, well-manicured home looked like something out of a magazine.

"Maybe I should've gone to school for public relations

and Marketing. Shoot, then I could have something this big to sleep in."

"Well, your house is pretty big too. I don't know what you are talkin' about. Plus, this house comes with big bills."

"Well, this is like... a million-dollar home. You sure you don't have any playboy bunnies in there?"

"Ha-Ha. Very funny."

We went inside, and it was well-furnished. I mean it looked almost better than the furniture in my house. Maybe a woman decorated for him, an ex-girlfriend or wife. it was too early in the game to be that nosy. Cole instantly ran me a bubble bath. Popped some champagne and gave me a glass.

"I want you to take it easy and enjoy yourself. I know you've had a rough day and you need to relax. Call me if you need anything." After he was done, and I was situated. He walked toward the door. "I promise I am not trying to set you up. I know how you are probably thinkin'."

"You are right. At this point, yo ass is showin' off. You had me questioning my safety around you." I was not scared at all. I had been soaking in the tub already for about 10 minutes.

The next morning. I woke up to breakfast in bed. I figured if Cole didn't kill me in my sleep, it was safe to eat his breakfast.

My phone buzzed on the nightstand on the charger. I figured Cole must have plugged it up while I was sleep. I slid the silk sheets off me. I had six missed calls from Marshall. I wasn't worried about getting home, but I knew I had to. I had ten missed calls from Lori. I even had two missed calls from Maxine.

I had tons of unread text messages. I tossed my phone

on the side of me on the bed where Cole sat.

"So, what do you want to do today?" he stared at me with a smile stretched from ear to ear.

I smiled wistfully, "I think I better get home. Everyone is worried about me."

When I got to the house, I went into our room, and there were fresh flowers on the nightstand with break-fast. He hadn't cooked for me in forever. Are you fucking serious?! I threw the flowers and breakfast in our small trashcan that sat by the door.

"I've been calling and texting you. What happened?" He stormed in the room. He glanced at his peacemaking gift in the garbage.

"You are looking really nervous, Marshall. What do you think happened?" I walked toward our on-suite and turned on the water and ran a relaxing bath.

"I don't know. That's why I asked." He followed behind me.

"Nothing happened. The officers just asked me ques-tions. I told they ass it wasn't me. They didn't believe me, so they kept me overnight thinking they would get a con-fession." I lied.

"Do you have time to talk? I want to talk about us and what's going to happen between us. I am sorry, and I know I took it too far this time."

"This time? Really? What about the other times—" I poured bubble bath, and I climbed into the bathtub.

"What about the firm? How is that going?"

"You really want to talk about the firm now, huh?" I turned my bath water off. "How about we talk about this another time. I need to relax."

He walked out of the bathroom. "If that's how you want it to be."

"No, I want you to stop cheating, but since that can't happen. Get the fuck out." I yelled and waved my hand dismissively.

The next day there was more breakfast. Then the next day, it was even more breakfast and lunch. Next day breakfast, lunch, and dinner. Attached were little notes that read, Please forgive me. I know I really fucked up this time. Every message I got; I threw them in my trashcan with all the other little sorry ass pieces of paper. A couple of days went by, and I didn't say a word to him. The last message I got from him read, 'Will you please go out to dinner with me tonight?' I circled no. After the rejection, he ran me a bubble bath with champagne. I loved a good bubble bath with champagne. I accepted the bath although he was too late because Cole already hit that spot. Even after the bath and champagne I didn't say a word to him.

I woke up to three new expensive dresses stretched across the bed. Marshall sat at the end of the bed with a puppy dog face. That face used to make me fall for anything. "All of this because I caught yo ass cheating." My hand swung back and then forward across his face. My hand started to hurt instantly.

"Man, what's all that for? I am trying to be nice, and you smackin' me and shit. That's not cool."

"The fuck you mean...what's not cool is that you are a cheating ass dog." I hung my new dresses in the closet. I wasn't giving those dresses back he owed me.

Even though I fucked Cole more than I should. I still felt betrayed. Marshall started it and has always tested me, now its his turn to take the test.

"I'm trying to get past that," he begged.

"Anyway, where the hell you gettin' all this money to

buy this shit with?"

"C'mon now. I did just graduate and it's been weeks. I do have a job now. Oh, but you didn't bother to ask me about."

"Man, fuck yo job."

"See, Ronnie. That's the reason I would sneak around."

I stood waiting for the rest of his sob story.

"Because I never thought I was good enough for you," he continued. "I never had a lot of money, and it seemed like you were takin' care of everything. I didn't feel like a man. So, I didn't feel needed."

My phone buzzed on the bed. I walked over to see who it was. Lori's name lit up in the display, but I ignored it. I hadn't talked to her that much since Marshalls graduation. She was always worried about me and called me every day because she thought I would kill Marshall.

To make it seem like everything was still all good between us. I had sex with Marshall. "You like that?"

"Yes, this is what I needed, daddy." I rolled my eyes, unpleased. Maybe he didn't feel like a man. That was still no reason to cheat, though. But I was going to keep it going like it was. I didn't want him to know that I was getting dick somewhere else and if I don't fall for his little trick, he would have most definitely caught on. I would fall for the Okie Doke through the years, so I couldn't just change the routine. I kept him from wondering. I would continue to let him buy me shit with his new job and make him pay these bills.

"I'm bout to cum... I'm cumming," he grunted.

"Oh cum...cum," I screamed while rolling my eyes, unbothered.

He stepped out of the room and walked into the bathroom.

CHAPTER 7

Scott & Williams

Two Months Later

*H*ey Ronnie, how has everything been? I am flying to New York this weekend, and I wanted to know if you wanted to come along. I got in touch with Scott and Williams, LLC, and they said we could take a tour around, and maybe you can take some notes. Great opportunity. Let me know.
Cole.

I've been thinking about Cole ever since he sent me that text two days ago. I just came off my period, and I bought an ovulation test. Marshall and I tried again the night before when we saw a happy face appear on display. I stayed positive and knew we should continue to give it a try and continue to work on us. When he said he hasn't felt like a man it ran through my mind over and over. He had never given me this much attention before, well, I mean like we've never had a conversation with him actually talking about his feelings. I guess a job and a little money can change a man. I always ran back to him every time he cheated. When was I going to get enough, though?
Phone buzzed.

Cole's name lit up in display.

Hey, I don't know if you got my last text, but let me know as soon as possible. Thanks!

I didn't reply. I honestly didn't know what to say. I walked toward the kitchen, and Marshall was leaning over the island on his phone. I stared at him from a distance, and there was that unfaithful smile once again. I walked closer to the entryway of the kitchen. I stood back behind the wall and watched him. I stuck the side of my head out more and extended my ear so I could hear better.

"You are so funny," a soft-spoken girl said.

"Ha-ha. I'm funny, but you are fine."

"I miss you so much," the girl said in a very alluring way.

"I miss you too. When am I going to see you again?" He chuckled.

I knew it was too good to be true. All that shit about not being a man. Blah. Blah. Blah. Having a job just meant more hoes and more clothes. I had been thinking about Cole, and, at the same time, I ignored his text for an asshole that didn't even have the decency to wait until I left the house to do his hoe calls. "Who are you talking to?" I strolled into the kitchen.

He hung up the phone without a bye, farewell, or anything. "Oh, no one. Calling in a delivery." His face looked so sincere.

He was just one lying ass motherfucker. Wouldn't trust him to save his own damn life. I was sure he thought I believed that. "What did you order?'

"Well, I wasn't ordering anything. I was confirming an order." Marshall lied.

He musta been ordering some ass. "Well, I guess it's

none of my business since you are giving me such short, weak ass answers. Good day, Marshall." When I got back to our room, I grabbed the picture of us that sat on the nightstand and threw it against the wall. It shattered and glass flew everywhere.

All the things I could be doing right now, and I am sitting here wasting my time. I grabbed my phone from our bed.

Yes, Cole, I would love to go. But what I really wanted to say was yes, I would love to go so we can fuck, suck, eat, dance, talk, and laugh, but I was going to make sure all of that happened anyway. *Also, can I come to stay with you for the rest of the week?* I needed to get away from Marshall as soon as possible before I hurt him.

Sure, of course, what time do you think you'll be able to come?

Be there in about an hour or two if you let me.

Yeahhh. C'mon.

Marshall walked the room with a smile on his face until he saw me throwing a things in my Louie suitcase. I walked past him like he wasn't even standing there.

"Where are you going?" he said hesitantly.

"I have to go out of town for the week for a business trip." I continued to throw toiletries into my bag.

"You didn't say anything about this before," he said confused.

"Maybe because we haven't had a chance to talk because you were out there cheatin'," I yelled. I had to get myself together and stop showing him that I cared. I knew he saw that as my weakness. "Never mind, I am telling you now I am going to Los Angeles for a conference meeting." I couldn't tell him that I was going to New York. He would've hopped on a flight and tried to surprise me. He had money now. I grabbed my bag and walked out. Drove around the corner to Cole's house. So convenient and scary at the same time. I parked in his garage.

Cole met me at the door. He looked fine as wine in his muscle shirt and basketball shorts. Skin smooth and smelled like he just got out of the shower. He grabbed my bag and carried them to the guestroom. I followed behind him. We got to the room, and there sat on the bed a tray with a mimosa and strawberries.

"Damn, I didn't know I was at a resort." He knew how to make a mad woman feel good.

"Welcome to Resort Coles," he chuckled.

Phone rang. Marshall's name lit up in the display.

"Hello?"

Marshall concerned. "Where are you?" I wished we could've talked about this more. What day are you coming back?"

He was so funny. He was trying to act like he is concerned. He was asking all the right questions for all the wrong answers. I figured he just wanted to know to see how long Casey could stay. "I'll be back when I get back." I hung up the phone and looked at Cole.

"So, what happened? Why did you need to come over?"

"No real reason. It's just that Marshall is at it again. I thought he would've stopped by now." I sat down in the chair next to the bed. I crossed my legs and put my head into the palm of my hand. "Sorry, I've been ignoring you. I just wanted things to go back to the way it was. You know. Try to fix my marriage again."

"It's cool." He walked over, sat at the edge of the bed. "I understand."

"How are you this understanding? Wait, is it really

okay for me to be here? You are not going to have a woman come over in the middle of the night, are you? I don't want to fuck things up for you," I said in a joking , but I was super serious.

"If you believe it or not, Ronnie. You are the only woman I fuck with. Not saying that I like you being married. But I am trying to keep things real simple. I've been hurt before. So, I just stick to myself. Plus, you are a client, and you are going to make me some money soon."

"So, I am just a business deal to you, huh?"

"I told you, Ronnie, you are married. I am not the type to come in between something like this. Now what we've been doing, I have never done before, and I wasn't trying to do, but I honestly want the best for you." I could see the hurt in his eyes. "But anyway, would you like me to make your plate? I made steak and potatoes."

"Yes, I am so hungry. I would love a plate. You didn't cook because I was coming over, did you?" I giggled, hoping I changed his mood.

"Mwah Ha Ha Ha, that's exactly the reason why I cooked." He rubbed his hands together mimicking birdman.

He walked out of the room. I didn't know what to think about more; the fact that I was constantly getting cheated on or the fact that I think I was falling in love with Cole. I asked God to take the wheel. The guest room he had me settled into was just as lovely as the rest of the house. It was a little dusty, but it smelled great. I tried to turn on the television, but the remote didn't work. I banged the remote control in the palm of my hand. I took the batteries out and rubbed them together. I put them back in and voilà, it worked.

"You wanna come down and eat?" He yelled from

downstairs.

"Yes, I am on my way down." On my way down, I noticed a picture on his wall. The lady looked familiar, but I wasn't sure where I might have known her from.

The sound of the alarm woke me, and it was time to head to the airport.

I was so nervous, and all I could do was think about how exciting it would be to intermingle with one of the world's biggest firms. I couldn't believe that Cole was giving me the opportunity. If I weren't already married, I would have been begging him to marry me.

I walked past the kitchen. "Hold on. Hold on." His abrupt voice grabbed my attention. He passed me a cup of coffee. "Can't have a productive day without this." I looked at him in amazement. How can someone be so thoughtful? He grabbed my bags and ran toward the door.

"Hold on, hold on." I motioned my index finger for him to come to me.

He dropped my bags on the floor where he stood and walked toward me. I began to kiss him, and he kissed me back. He pushed me against the wall and took his jacket off. I helped unbutton his shirt and his pants instantly after. He pulled down his briefs and lifted my skirt. He moved my panties to the side and pulled my right leg up. The heels that I had on gave him significant leverage to slide his anaconda inside of me. We had an awesome quickie, and then it was out the door to the airport. We didn't talk about what just happened back at his place. We just glanced and smiled at each other all the way to the airport. The way Cole looked at me was nothing like any of the looks Marshall had ever given me. The look of admiration, joy, and pleasure was something I'd yearned for.

We arrived in New York City. People walked by with smiles on their faces. The weather there was nothing like it was back home. Something I would've had to get used it. We grabbed something to eat before heading to the hotel.

The next day we grabbed breakfast and headed out to Scott and William, LLC Law firm.

"Are you ready for an exciting day? You are going to meet your competiti—"

"He is not my competition. He is my inspiration."

"How much do you know about this firm?" We walked swiftly. The nervousness in me wished we slowed down, but we had to keep up with the crowd walking around us.

"Well, I know that the company is one of the biggest to have ever been in business since 1965. I know that Mr. Williams is married. I never really tried to figure out how the name Scott was related, though. I know that he is worth millions, if not billions. He has been in the newspapers and has gotten many blessings from his clients. I know a little more, but that's about it."

"Well, that's impressive." We took a couple more steps forward, and by the time I looked up. "We are here, Miss Lawson. What do you think?"

"I think…I think… I think it's beautiful." I couldn't get the words out. "I cannot believe I am actually in New York in front of a firm that I have admired ever since forever." We walked inside. Cole held the door open and walked behind me. The firm was so elegant. Workers dressed to impress. Not a stain or wrinkle in sight. I danced in a circle to try to capture all of what the firm had to offer. "Excuse Me," I said, almost bumping into an employee.

"Oh, you're fine. That was my mistake." The employee said as she swiftly walked by. This visit was a dream come true.

"I want my firm to be just like this, if not better," I said to Cole.

"No worries. It will be Miss. Lawson," he had been calling me Miss Lawson like I wasn't married. I appreciated that.

We walked over to the elevators.

"We don't have to check-in?"

"No, we are fine. I told the company we would be here by this time."

It was kind of weird because, at a gorgeous place like that, I would have thought we would have had to check-in.

"At my firm, we are going to check everyone in at the front desk for sure. That's just how a lot of businesses operate. Maybe they do things differently in New York."

"Umm. Somewhat."

We headed to the eleventh floor. "Are you ready to see what goes down in these offices?" He smiled.

"Yes, I am so ready." I almost pissed myself. If only he knew how hard my heart was beating, he would be taking me to the hospital and not to the eleventh floor. My palm started to sweat. My legs felt faint. I turned and kissed him on the cheek

"What was that for?" He asked.

"You will find out soon enough." I winked my eye. I was going to fuck Cole so well. The elevator opened. We walked toward a closed door at the end of the hall. On the nametag, it said Mr. Williams. We walked inside without knocking.

"Good Morning pop!" He walked over to Mr. Williams, who met him halfway and gave him a tight hug. They released each other and readjusted their clothes.

"Glad you had a safe trip. How is everyone treating you out there?" Mr. Williams walked back to the seat at his desk.

"Everything is fine." Cole motioned with his hand for me to sit in the front of Mr. Williams's desk. He pulled the chair out, and when I sat down, he helped push my chair up.

"You know your mother misses you." He took a sip from his coffee. It smelled so good. Unlike something I've ever smelled before. I hope he offered me some.

"Yes, I know. Mom still likes to treat me like a child."

She is proud of you, son, and you know that you are her baby." He looked over at me and smiled. "Well, that's for another day," he looked over at Cole and then back at me. "So, this must be the young lady you were telling me about? The young lady who wants to shadow me. She's beautiful."

Omg, did you say shadow?
So, I had to follow him around?
For how long? What was I supposed to do?
My legs got weak.

"Is she the one?"

"Yes, she is the one that will be shadowing you."

"No, I mean the one, the one? You haven't brought a girl around in an awfully long time."

"No pop. Miss. Lawson is just a friend."

"Hmmm. If you say so, but if you bring someone so far out to shadow me on your birthday, then Miss. Lawson must be special."

Did he say birthday? What was going on?
I didn't know it was his birthday.
I also didn't know that Mr. Williams was his father.
I didn't know anything about him.

Cole looked toward me. "No. It's not like that, but yes, this is the young lady who will be shadowing you. Her name is Ronnie, and she is brilliant."

"Oh, my competition. Nice to meet you. Miss—"

"Lawson, it's Miss Lawson."

"Wow, with that last name, you were born to be in this field, huh?

"I never really thought about it like that." I pondered.

"But, okay, now that we all know each other. I will take her for a bite to eat, and I will bring her back to get the day started," Cole said.

"Yeah, son, that's sounds like a plan." He smiled at me again with his beautiful veneers.

Cole slid my chair back and grabbed my hand to help me up. We walked out of the office.

Screaming, "Why didn't you tell me that Mr. Williams from Scott & Williams is your dad."

"Well, I wanted to keep it a secret. I don't tell everyone everything. I still have a couple of friends who still don't know, and I just don't care to share. Plus, you never asked."

"But... you're a millionaire, sir!"

"Call it what you want. I worked hard to get to where I am and although I could call and ask for anything I wanted, I didn't. I wanted to do everything on my own. But, let me not front I got a huge graduation gift that kind of helped. Ha-Ha"

I looked at him in awe.

"Oh yeah, Grand Ru is my resturant. That's why I like to

cook so much."

"Cole, are you serious?"

"Umm huh." He shook his head up and down.

"Wooow, but besides that, you didn't even tell me that it's your birthday today."

"Yeah. Speaking of that, my birthday party is tonight. May I have the honor of taking you as my date?"

"Whaattt? I didn't pack any party clothes. I can't go. I am not about to go around your family looking a mess."

"Nevermind that, I'll stop by the store and get you something while you are with my pops. What size are you about a size eight?"

"Yes, where did you learn your sizes? When you shop for other women?"

"Wow, not really. My mom is about your size. I buy things for her all the time."

"Right, blame it on your mom." I hoped he was telling the truth about only shopping for his mom because it felt good when he said things like that.

Cole and I arrived at the airport. Although I didn't want to leave my dream world, I hurried home. I couldn't stop thinking about Coles' birthday party. He was the man of the hour, and he made me feel like the hour's woman, unlike Marshall. Marshall had always been the type to hang around his friends having dick debates. Rather than showing me a good time. When I walked through the door, Marshall ran to me and wrapped his arms around me so tight my airway circulation started to cut off. My backbones began to crack. I immediately pushed him off.

"Where have you been? I've been calling and text-ing you, and you weren't answering. I was worried. Are you okay?" I walked over the dining table. "I am glad you made it back safely, man...what happened?" He continued.

"Well, story short, umm, I lost my phone." I placed my bags in the chair that sat by our kitchen island. "I was so upset. I don't know, one minute, I am grabbing my luggage, and the next, I was looking for my phone. But thank goodness someone returned it to me." I lied. "Apparently, I left it in the bathroom. I am glad I got it back tho."

"Me too. It's rare when someone turns in a phone."

"I know right, but other than that how did you enjoy your alone time?"

"It was okay. I just wondered around worried. I was about to put in a missing person report, but your mom said to hold off. I guess she must have known something."

Yeah, I talked to her and told her to tell your dumb ass to calm down. "Yes, but I am back no more worrying, right?" I asked him hoping he knew it was a rhetorical question. I wanted to change the subject.

"Well, now that you are back. We can go try and make a baby." He started to kiss me on my neck.

"Sounds like a plan. Meet me upstairs. I need to take a quick shower." I had to wash off the airplane bathroom sex smell. I looked down and rubbed my stomach. "Tonight's the night."

After we had sex, Marshall sat up on the side of the bed.

"That was something special, girl."

I aligned my back with the headboard. "Yeah, I know right." He walked over to my side of the bed and got on one knee. "Ronnie, I am sorry for everything I put you through. I just want us to start over and make it right. Will you marry me again, Ronnie?"

I was in shock. My mind didn't know what to say, but

my mouth said, "Yes...yes...yes," I yelled. I grabbed Marshall by the sides of his face and brought it toward me for a big kiss on the lips. I just needed to hear that he wanted to make it right. I was in love all over again.

CHAPTER 8

Meet My Husband

Everything had been going well ever since Marshall promised to be more compassionate. I hadn't talked to Cole in two and a half months. Of course, he tried to call me, but he started to get a clue when I wouldn't pick up or return his calls. I was in the process of finding another person to help finish what I started with my firm. Things had been well until I walked over to Marshall's phone to put it on the charger. Hey, Baby lit up okay display from 'Main'. Some things just didn't change. I opened the text messaging screen.

"Hey, baby. You want to go out to dinner?" Marshall said, walking back in our room. I connected his phone to the charger without reading any further.

"Yes, I sure do."

"I made a reservation Mad Cave," he said.

Mad Cave was a popular restaurant in the Hills. Tourist enjoyed it there. I threw on my black slim fit dress and red bottom heels. That was what I usually wore when I went on dates with Marshall. He was not impressed when I switched up, and it was the last outfit he has ever complimented me on. I barely did anything to my hair. I wasn't really in the mood, and I didn't even think about it. I was too hangry, though.

There was a fresh bouquet of roses and a bottle of champagne sitting on top of a spotless white linen tablecloth upon our arrival. He tried to make it a grand date.

"This job called me, and I was thinking about accepting. Maybe I could work there and still look for another job, well somewhere I would want to work," Marshall rambled before we were even seated.

"Oh yeah, what job is this?" I asked. I was sure he wanted me to ask. I wasn't really interested in knowing I wanted to eat in silence.

Marshall continued to ramble on. One thought after another. I don't even think he stopped to gasp for air or even took his eyes out of the menu to notice if I had fallen asleep or walked away. By that time, I had already had three glasses of champagne. I crossed my legs, straightened and pulled my dress down.

At that exact moment, there was an indistinct outburst of laughter behind me. I looked around for any type of enjoyment. I turned around and to my most pleasant surprise, Cole sat there with a group of guys and girls. He was staring at my table. I turned my head towards Marshall, and he hadn't even raised his head from the dinner section of the menu. I grabbed the champagne bottle and took a huge gulp.

Marshall finally looked up to search for the waitress and caught me wiping the dripping champagne from my chin. "Is everything okay?" he said, puzzled.

"Yes, I'm—"

Marshall interrupted, "Then I got another offer to be a morning pharmacist," he continued. I didn't know what to do or how to act. I was sure Cole felt some type of way about me ignoring him out of the blue. I looked over my left shoulder to get another peek at Cole, and he was no longer sitting in his seat.

A firm hand rested on my tensed shoulder.

"Ronnie, OMG! It's surprising to see you here." Behind my right shoulder a voice overpowered Marshall's conversation. The scent of the cologne smelled way too familiar.

It couldn't have been.

It wasn't.

Cole?!

I turned around slowly. "Heyyyyyy, how are you? It's a pleasure seeing you here also." I turned back towards Marshall, who was bluntly confused. I took another gulp from the bottle. I couldn't believe that I put myself in that position.

"This must be your husband. Nice to meet you." Cole extended his hand for a handshake. "Bastard," he mumbled.

"I'm sorry, I didn't catch that," Marshall inquired.

Cole released his hand, "Oh, I didn't say any—"

"Well, Marshall, this is Cole," I interrupted.

"You look oddly familiar, Cole. Have we met somewhere before?" Marshall tapped his two finger on his chin.

"No, I can't say that we have."

"You look like someone." Marshall contemplated. "Did you go to....? You know what, baby. He looks like that uber driver who picked you up that one time. You know the night of my graduation reception," he implied. "Oh... you know what. You're a police officer, right." Marshall stared me in my eyes for confirmation.

"No, I am not a police officer or a driver. I am your wife's future partner. I mean, I was her business partner." Cole smirked.

"Nah. Nah. Nah. I'm sure you're a police office,' he said

confidently.

"Okay then, Marshall. If you think so, but I am trying to tell you this is the guy who is helping me start my own firm."

"Okay then." His mouth twisted into a sardonic smile. "How's the firm going anyway?" Marshall took a sip of champagne and looked down at his phone.

I waited for Cole to answer, but instead, he rolled his eyes. "Well, it was nice to meet you. Ronnie, I'll see you soon to discuss more details about your amazing work and interest. You're doin' your thang girl. You'll always have my support even after our business is over with." He winked.

"Okay, I'll see you soon."

Cole walked away. My eyes followed his firm ass. Marshall was still looking through his phone.

Text tone. Cole name lit up in display.

Meet me by the bathroom withcho fine ass.

Yes, Daddy. Whatever you want.

"I'll be right back. Order some more champagne." I rushed from the table.

"Where are you going so fast?"

"To the bathroom," I yelled. I bumped into the waitress on my sprint to the bathroom, she almost spilled red wine all over me. "I am sorry," I yelled to the waitress. I continued to sprint.

A pair of hands snatched me into the bathroom. Gently placed me on the wall. Cole lifted my dress and put his fingers between my second pair of fat lips. He kissed my neck and put his other hand around my neck. "Daddy... Daddy...Daddddy," I screamed as he penetrated his fingers in me. With the hand he gripped my neck with, he unzipped his pants and pulled out his giant monster. "Yesss," I yelled. He put his hand across my opened mouth. His hips rolled and bounced me up and down on his anaconda at a steady pace. I rocked back and forth. I couldn't help but to scratch his back through his finely ironed shirt. He pulled out, turned me around, bent me over the sink, and gave it to me the right way, rough and hard at a fast pace. My ass shook while smacking his thighs. He breathed faster and faster. The basin shook loose. I exploded.

Next, I did something that I didn't regret. I got on my knees and sucked that monster dry. I put my mouth around and laid my warm tongue horizontally under his dick. I sucked on his thick head and then put it all in my mouth. I felt the pressure of his vein on my lips; his monster got more demanding and more abundant. I slurped, sipped, and licked. He pulled his dick out of my mouth and exploded. I opened my eyes; his seeds dripped down my chest.

"I tried not to get it on you, my bad," he explained.

"It's okay. I appreciate it tho." I pulled my dress down and wiped my red smudged lipstick from my face. The toilet tissue was filled with his monster slim after I wiped my chest clean. I escaped the men's bathroom. I made it back to my seat.

"You know what... I think we should call it a night," Marshall said before I could sit back down.

I slide my chair closer to the table. "Okay," I replied. Cole sat at his table and looked at me from the corner of his eyes. Marshall paid the bill and we left.

In the car on the way home, Marshall seemed intense "You know what I am just going to tell you," he blurted out. "Casey is pregnant, and I am the father. But I don't want to be with her. I want to be with you."

Everything went black. I thought I was moving back-ward; I took several deep breaths as my pulse rate in-creased.

Did he just say?

Am I hearing things?

Is he serious?

"Ronnie, I said Casey is pregnant," he repeated and waved his right hand across my face.

I turned in his direction, anger took over me, and with-out any more delay, I roared, "You just fucked that up any chances of being with me, don't you think." I grabbed the steering wheel, and I turned it to the right. We were headed toward the side of the road into a ditch.

His hand gripped the wheel. The steering wheel barely budged.

I grabbed my purse, swung it around with full force, and aimed it at his head. My goal was to knock his head off his shoulders, but he ducked. The car swerved, and he lifted his head instantly. When he did that, his cheek lined up right along with the palm of my hand.

WHAAM!

His head jerked, and a speck of blood flew from his cheek. His mouth dropped. He placed his hand on his cheek to comfort it. My wedding ring had cut him.

I rubbed the palm of my hand and fixed my ring.

"What is wrong with you, Ronnie, damn?" he shouted. "It's not like you can give me any kids."

WHAAM!

"Oh, so we are going to take it there, mo-ther-fuck-er, I am your wife. Just because I can't give you kids doesn't mean you go out and have kids with someone else you fucker. Then you have the nerve to sit here and ask what's wrong with me?... What wrong with me? No, what the fuck is wrong with you?"

He stared out the front window with a face only a mother could feel sorry for. He held his lips where my smack landed the second time.

"Whats wrong, what's wrong with me? What the fuck is wrong with you?" I continued, "But, yeah, I couldn't get pregnant fast enough for you, huh?" I muffed him. His head was seconds from hitting the driver's side door window. "Take me the fuck home, yo clown ass." I gagged and vomit flew everywhere. "Hurry the hell up. I have to lay down," I yelled.

He reached on the backseat and grabbed a bag. He handed it to me, and I continued to throw up.

"Man, fuck that bag." I threw the bag at him when I finished.

He caught it. "Ugh, really, Ronnie?" He threw the bag in the backseat.

We pulled into the driveway. "Tell me a bitch that's gonna do you better?" I challenged him. The car hadn't even come to a complete stop before I jumped out.

"Casey obviously," he replied, coldly.

I bent down, picked up a tree branch, and swung it into his car, shattering his front window. "FUCK YOU!" I flipped him the bird and walked inside the house.

My Louie bag was full of clothes by the time Marshall walked into our closet. "And where the hell do you think you're going?"

"That's funny. You just told me you got a bitch pregnant, and you are worried about me now...now, you real stupid? Get out of here." I ran to the bathroom, but I vomited before I made it to the toilet. "What the fuck? Did you try to poison me?" I yelled from the bathroom.

"What the hell are you talking about?"

"I can't believe those two gulps of champagnes got me like this. You know what. Take yo raggedy ass in the guest room." Tears fell down my face uncontrollably. I couldn't understand how someone could be so cold-hearted to the woman who had been there for him through everything.

I knew I wouldn't get a good sleep that night, and on top of that, I could barely stand or walk a straight line without staggering. I finally made it to my bed, after an hour of sitting on the bathroom floor crying. I texted Cole.

Can I come over? I am not feeling well.

Yes, you can always come over. What's wrong?

I feel sick.

What? You want me to take you to the hospital.

No, I'll be fine. I just want to come over and lay with you.

The doors are open, beautiful.

Thanks, Cole.

It's all good.

I rolled over on my side and used my right arm to push me in a sitting position. I grabbed my overnight bag that sat on the bottom of the bed. I looked at myself in my mirror sliding door.

Was I that bad of a person?

Was I not enough?

Why did I have to go through this?

Who would have known that I could hurt so bad?

I walked down our long hallway past the guest room, where Marshall was still sleeping. I placed my hand on the door's frame and stared at him and waited for an explanation. There was none. He was who he was.

How could someone make you feel so loved and so undesirable at the same time?

"Let me help you with your bags," Cole said as he grabbed my left hand to help lift me from my seat. "I made you some breakfast. I hope you can eat." He interlocked our arms and walked me to the door.

"I feel much better. Maybe the fresh air helped." I rubbed my empty stomach.

"Or me?!" His dimpled smile felt like medicine.

"Yeah, or you." I smiled back. I wished I was half as enticing as Cole was. If I were, I probably wouldn't have been in that predicament to begin with.

"Your eyes are hazel today. So, what's wrong? He asked. He grabbed my bag while holding the door open so I could lead the way.

"What do you mean?" I walked over to his three-seating couch with two pillows propped in the middle.

"Your eyes turn hazel when something wrong," he informed.

"Oh, really." I paused and gave it some thought. "Welp, do you want the story in detail or..." I placed my hand's downs for support before falling onto his low comfy couch.

"Yes, in detail, will be fine." He grabbed a pillow from the middle of the couch and sat it against the armrest. He patted the cushion for me to lay my head. He sat down and turned his head toward giving me his full attention.

I laid my head on the pillow, "Marshall cheated a lot. He thought I never knew about it. I wouldn't even tell him I knew. But I was always sick to my stomach once I found out. He wouldn't show me affection or any attention. I would be ill, and he would say maybe you need to eat, but he wouldn't make me anything to eat. Maybe you need to take a long bath, but he wouldn't run my bathwater. Maybe I needed to rest, but he wouldn't fix the bed.

Tears welled up in my eyes. "He had no idea that I knew he was cheating, and the worst part he didn't even care enough to find out. I knew he was done with one girl when he started talking to another girl."

Cole wiped the tears from my eyes with his index.

"But she didn't last long, and to this day he doesn't know that I knew, and I don't know why I've never confronted him. But since I met you, I guess it gave me the strength to stand my ground and face both him and his chick. The old me would've acted like none of that happened at the graduation. I would've acted like I didn't hear or see anything and maybe just gotten sick again, but when a woman's fed up. You know the rest."

"Ronnie, sometimes you have to take a step back and ask yourself is it worth going through the pain. You have people who love you." He slid my hair behind my ear. Cole smiled, leaned across me, and pressed a kiss on my forehead.

"Why are you so good to me?

My mom always said, 'you lose a person the same way you got him. They will always be good to you for the first six months', but I never listened.

"I am not trying to get over on you if that's what you think. I believe things will work themselves out. I don't think about how nice I am to you. I just give you the same energy that you give me. We've known each other for a while now, and I don't want to see you hurt girl." He pressed another kiss on my forehead.

I looked over at him and smiled.

"But to think about it. I do treat you better than all the girls I've ever talked to in the past. But I want you to know that even if we are not together, I got you. I want you to know that it's better men out here. Especially for someone who is as smart, motivated, and as beautiful as you are. Period Pooh. Ain't that what y'all be saying?" He laughed.

"You're remarkably interesting, Cole. Very hilarious. But, no I don't say that." I lied and laughed so hard I had to hold my stomach before it burst in half. Tears fell from my eyes, and it was more than a cry from a laugh. I was hurt. My body hurt, my stomach hurt, my mind hurt, my heart hurt. "Why me? Why?" I yelled, shouted, stumped the cushions on the couch.

Cole leaned over to catch me before I fell to the floor. When I opened my eyes from crying, Cole wiped some more of my tears away. Once my eyes were free from weeping. My eyes looked into Cole's pretty gray eyes. A dark object appeared in my peripheral vision. Cole had pulled his dick outside of his jeans and laid it on his left thigh. "You want this dick or not?" he asked.

"Yess." I wiped the rest of the tears from my eyes. "Make love to me, Cole."

He scooped me up into his strong arms before heading up the stairs to his master bedroom. I sucked on his smooth, gentle neck. His bedroom door was opened, and he strolled right inside and sat me at the end of his white sheeted bed.

I reached down to grab his waistband and pulled his pants down to his ankles. I pressed my lips on his shaft on the way down.

He slipped his Gucci flip flops off, and his pants followed. He had nothing under his jeans. His dick hung mid-thigh.

I slowly undressed while he stroked his dick. I licked

my finger and circled my breast, landing on my hard-
pointy nipples. I turned over, put both knees in the bed,
and crawled toward the headboard, but before I could get
there, Cole crawled in the bed right after me and pressed
his fingertips against the middle of my back and pushed
me down gradually.

"Ohhhh."

He leaned his lean body on mines. I felt his dick between my cheeks. His firm hand caressed my thighs, hips,
and sides up to my mouth. I licked his finger, and he
licked it right after. My heart started to beat faster

"Mmmmm..."

"Are you alright, beautiful?" he asked.

Before I could respond, he disappeared. He licked a
trail from just below my buttocks, around to my hips.
He continued to lick a path right above my buttocks, following my spine ending with a kiss behind my left ear.

Goosebumps raced across my body. My pussy mois-
tened and throbbed uncontrollably in sync with my
heartbeat. He flipped me over.

"You like that shit?" he whispered. He licked right
above my pelvis and blew cold air on it.

I raced my fingers between my legs. He grabbed them
and threw them off to the side. I jumped up, preparing to
take his dick in my mouth. He threw me down. "I got this,
shorty." He placed his long thick fingers in me.

"Ohhhhh... ahhhh...But...but...I want to suck your
dick."

He took more inches of me with his finger.

"You like when daddy do that?" he raised his eyebrow.
He removed his fingers and caressed my breast. He circled
my tense nipples and softly pinched the tip. He glided his
fingers across the crease of my bust around to my back

and met my buttocks. He smacked and palmed my ass cheek. "No, need to suck my dick. I got you today." He disappeared, and he pulled my thighs apart and placed one on each of his shoulders. He opened my lips with the tip of his tongue, exposing my clit to him. He seized my clit into his mouth and took one big suck before blowing a cool breeze across my pussy. My buttocks clenched together, and I lifted slightly off the bed.

He used his index fingers to separate my lips. He placed my clit into his mouth once again. I gasped and bit my bottom lip at the feel of him sucking me at a steady pace.

I grabbed and tugged on his ears and massaged his head.

He glided his tongue into my vagina opening and by that time, I wanted him. I pulled his head up, and his sexy muscular body crawled up to me like a lion creeping up on his prey.

"Do you want this dick?" he barked. "I said, do you want this dick?" He repeated.

"Yes, Zaddy...Yes, I do." I rubbed the back of his head.

I had not been home for a couple of hours. Still, Marshall didn't even have the decency to check on me. I stayed at Coles' another night.

Text tone. Lori name lit up in the display.

Hey Ronnie,

I stared at the message, not knowing what to text back.

I've been trying to call you. I haven't heard anything back. I wanted to know if you wanted to go out with Stephanie and me? Call me when you can.

Stephanie was our other cousin who I didn't see very

often. After she got married, she distanced herself from us. I don't know if it was her idea or her husband's.

I replied after careful thinking.

Hey Lori,

I can't come out right now. I haven't been in the best mood. I haven't told anybody, but I found out that Marshall got that girl from the graduation pregnant. I am mad as hell and as-tound because after all the shit I've been through with him, he does some shit like this. Like really?! I don't feel like talking right now. Call you soon.

I didn't wait for her to respond. I placed my phone in my overnight bag and laid down. I knew Lori would go off the walls with text messages and calls.

About an hour or two into watching one of my favorite movies, my phone started to rang and lite up.

A FaceTime call from Marshall was displayed on my phone, and I ignored it. My phone rang again, and I missed that call too. It must have been important if he called that many times. The third ring. I answered.

"Yeah, what do you want?"

"Why would you send Lori over here? I think she is try-ing to kill me," his voice cracked as he flipped the camera around on his phone. It was Lori with a knife in her hand. She walked toward Marshall.

I propped my upper body straight up in the bed. "Lori, nooooo. Please don't do it. Stop Lori, please," I screamed through the phone.

"Naw, fuck that," she yelled. "Bitch don't play with my cousin like that." She charged at Marshall, and the call dropped.

I jumped up out of bed quickly to searched for my pants and shoes. My heart was beating so loudly; it be-came deafening. Cole running in the bedroom was the last thing I saw before everything went black.

Beep...Beep...Beep

My eyes were heavy. I was groggy and shivered. I tried to open my eyes, but they wouldn't separate. They burned underneath my eyelids. My arms hurt. I forcefully tried to open and close my eyes until they started to peel apart, and I began to faintly see myself hooked up to two iv bags hanging from the port. The patient monitor was hooked up to the end of the big thick band around my lower arm. Paper crumbled, monitor beeped, doors opened and closed. I turned toward the spot where the paper sound was coming from, and it was Cole. He sat on the side of me in front of the tv and flipped through a magazine.

He turned to me. "Hey, you. How are you feeling?"

"How long have we been here?" My voice cracked. I could hardly talk.

"For a couple of ho—"

"Oh, no. Lori," I yelled. I yanked on my ivs. They didn't budge. I felt weak.

The nurses ran into the room. "Calm down. Is everything alright?"

"No. I have to see where Lori is," I said to Cole. I reached for my phone. There was no way I was able to get up and get it. It sat across the room on the table with my purse.

"You need to relax. You are in no condition to get yourself all roused up."

Cole sensed the urgency and gave me my phone. "What happened with Lori? Is that why I found you laid out?" he asked, concerned.

"You do know this man, right, miss?"

"Yes, I know him."

I had missed calls from Lori and a missed call from

Marshall.

Text tone. Lori's name in the display.

It's done.

I didn't want to text just in case it was incriminating, but I didn't want to call either, or she would've found out where I was, but I also didn't want her to worry.

Hey, I'll call you in a minute.

A text came back instantly.

Hey bitch I've been calling you. I just went over there to scare his ass. He is okay. He pissed himself, girl. Where are you? I want to give you the details. Are you okay? You weren't home, and you weren't with me. Where are you, and why haven't you called?"

I'm fine. I'll call you in a bit.

I was relieved.

"Is everything okay?" The nurse asked.

"It is now." I exhaled. I handed Cole my phone.

"Please make sure that she doesn't do that again." The nurse instructed Cole.

"Okay. Now that everything is okay, I need to collect some urine and blood from you. The doctor will be in here to explain everything to you," she explained.

After a couple of episodes of *Martin* and a much-needed laugh, the doctor walked in.

"Hello Mrs. Valentine, I am Doctor Peters. How are you feeling?"

"I prefer Miss. Lawson and I am feeling fine."

"I'm so sorry. Your chart says, Valentine. I apologize." He flipped the pages in his clipboard. "Noted. So, do you know why you are here?"

"No, I have no idea. I remember everything going black and waking up here."

"Okay, I'll get straight to the point. You are pregnant."

I woke up, and the doctor was standing over me. My shoulders were gently rubbed by Cole.

"Miss... is everything okay," the doctor asked.

"No, everything is not okay. Especially the fact that you just violated HIPPA."

"Oh..No...No...No miss, I am sorry. I'm sorry. I thought it was okay being that he is the one who rushed you in and sat her with you till you woke."

Cole smirked at the doctor. "Really doc? You just doing yo thang today, huh?"

"Wait, can you repeat what you said. I don't think I caught that." Please, God, do not let him repeat what I think he said.

"You are pregnant, Miss...Miss." He looked down at my paperwork. "Miss. Law--"

Everything went black again for the third time. "What is going on?" I asked both the doctor and Cole. "Did you say I am pregnant?"

"Yes!" they said in unison

"Please explain doctor," I begged,

"We checked your urine. Two pregnancy tests came back positive. That's probably why you fainted at your home. You overexerted yourself. When was your last period?"

"I am not sure, doc. Maybe a month or two ago. I've been so stressed. I haven't been able to keep track," I explained.

"Okay. Okay, we are going to go ahead and do an ultrasound. Is that okay?" The doctor asked.

"Yes, that's fine?" That moment was surreal. It felt good to be finally pregnant, but then again, it was the happiest and saddest day of my life. Casey and I were pregnant at the same time. I couldn't tell Marshall. I didn't plan on it either.

The nurse walked in with an ultrasound machine shortly after. "So, is this the father?" She looked at Cole.

"You all have a lot of unprofessional people who work here. You know that?" Cole retorted.

I laughed at Cole. "Honestly, girl, I am not sure," I said, avoiding eye contact with either one of them.

"Uh, okay, but between me and you depending on how far along you are, you can get a NIPP test, and it will tell you all your paternity details as early as seven weeks. Check into it if you want."

"I definitely will. Thanks, girl."

She rubbed gel across my belly and scanned my stomach. It was unbelievable. To finally see something so heart filing. I was disappointed Marshall wasn't sitting where Cole was. He should've been there watching our first ultrasound together.

"The baby's heart rate is fine, and you might be a little over a month pregnant. But I think you should go to your gynecologist for more details. She will tell you everything you need to know."

Tears of happiness flowed down my face like a river. Coles walked over and hugged me. "Yayyy, you're pregnant," he said happily. "No matter what happens. I got you," he reassured me.

"But if you still are uncertain, make an appointment as soon as possible. So, you can get the proper care," the nurse suggested.

"My head hurts so bad," I said to Cole.

"Yeah. All that damn crying you are doing," Cole laughed. "You don't have to cry tho. You and your husband will be just fine."

"Do you think I should go to the place the nurse was

talking about?"

"Do you have any doubts?"

"Well, of course, I do. Don't you?"

"Nah, I strapped up, and if I did have doubts. It wouldn't matter."

"Don't be like that, Cole."

Cole got up and stormed out of the room

"Cole," I yelled.

I was a pregnant woman!

CHAPTER 9

WHY NOW?

"I can't deal with what's going on," Cole said.

He drove me back to my house that night. He flipped on me and I honestly didn't know what got him so upset.

Hello. Early Detect Center. My name is Cathy. Who do I have the pleasure of speaking with?" a pleasant voice said on the other end of the phone.

Hi, my name is Ronnie.

Hi, how can I help you today, Ronnie?

I wanted to know how your faculty works.

I would be happy to give you the information you need. Would you like to schedule an appointment to come in and talk to a prenatal-paternity expert?

Yes, that would be fine.

Okay, I just need some information. What's your full name and date of birth?

My full name is Ronnie M. Lawson and my date of birth is June 23, 1986.

Do you know how many weeks you are?

No, I do not. I have an appointment in two days.

Okay, we can schedule an appointment for you to come in after your doctor's appointment. I'll schedule you for the day after. I have a three-thirty p.m. Will that be okay?

Yes, that's great.

Okay. See you then. We'll call one day before as a re-
minder. Thanks, and have a great day.

There were three steps. The first step was to set up an
appointment at a faculty near me, like a hospital or medical center to collect DNA. The next step was going to the
appointment to collect a blood sample from the mother
and a cheek swab from the possible father. I couldn't take
Marshall because I wasn't sure how I would tell him or
if I would tell him that I was pregnant. The last step is
to wait for about three business days to get results. This
process would go by faster than I thought. I didn't know
if I was happy or sad about having to go through this process. In my heart, it was Marshalls, but in my mind, it was
Coles.

I was surprised when Marshall walked into the room. I
was so into what I was doing that I didn't hear him come
in the house nor did I hear him come up the stairs. He
pulled his Nike hoodie over his head. I shut the computer
off as quickly as possible.

"You should always check the house to see if someone
is in here."

He jumped back, startled, and bumped his spine onto
the edge of the door. He hurried and pulled the rest of
his hoodie off his head. He looked over at me while I sat
up in the bed, watching *Martin*. "Damn, Ronnie. You can't
be scaring me like that. Why didn't you tell me you were
going to be here?"

"I didn't tell you because this is my house and I can go
and come as I please."

"I didn't mean it like that, Ronnie. I meant I could've
picked you up something to eat." He walked over to the
bathroom and started his shower.

"What are you showering for? You don't want me to smell that bitch on you?" I yelled, glowering at him.

"Ronnie, what are you talking about? I just came back from a run. I went over to the park."

"Yeah, I bet you did."

"Look, Ronnie. I don't want to fight. I honestly just want to talk. I want to start over."

"Start over? What do you mean start over?"

"I wanted to lay everything out on the table and tell you all that happened. Do you think you can deal with what I want to tell you without losing your head?"

"You better worry about losing your head." I gave him a chagrined smile.

The water stopped running, and he walked back in the room naked. His dick swung back and forth, bouncing off his thighs.

"You being naked is supposed to ease my mind about what you are about to say or...."

"I hoped so." He grabbed and yanked it.

"Well, it won't." It looked thick and juicy, though. Being pregnant had me horny as fuck. "Now, tell me what it is that you want to tell me."

He walked over to our dresser drawer and grabbed some briefs and a tank top. He got dressed as he walked back to lay in the bed beside me. "Now we can talk." He pulled the blanket over his legs just above his knees while my side of the blanket laid on my waistline.

"Now, where do you want me to start?"

"Ummm... I guess you can start with where you met her, duh." I gazed at him.

"I met her at the school's library. Next question."

"How long have known her, and what was your first intention."

"I've known her for five months."

"And...."

"And what?

"Look, see. We are not about to do this. If you aren't going to answer my questions, then get the hell out of my face."

"I am answering your questions. What do you mean?"

"You are going to tell me everything you want me to know. I want you to start from beginning to end. I am not going to play these games with you. Don't give me these simple ass answer. If you are going to play games, get the hell out of my face."

"Okay, okay...I met her about five months ago at the school's library. She walked up to me and told me that she had been checking me out in our chemistry class."

"That's all it took, huh?" I rolled my eyes.

"Ronnie!"

"Marshall!"

"Are you going to let me finish?"

"Boy, you better stop talking to me. I can say and do whatever I want, how about that." I cut my eyes at him.

"Don't start."

"Anyway."

"Yeah, anyway."

"Ronnie!" He threw his hands up.

"Marshall!"

"I got her number, and we started talking. That time that I came in mad and dirty is one of the times I was with her. We went out to eat, and someone busted my car windows out. That's why I started that argument."

"Yes, I remember." I smirked.

"She got pregnant after messing with her for two months. The third month she got pregnant and didn't know. So, when I found out. I told you. Well, I told you a little after because I didn't know how. She was just a fling, and I don't want to be with her. That's why I want to start over with you."

"When was the last time you saw her."

"I don't know. It's been a minute."

"Right, she is pregnant with your child, and you don't remember the last time you saw her." I pushed him out of the bed.

"Yes, Ronnie," he screamed from the floor. "It hurt because she got pregnant before you, and we've been trying for so long."

"It hurt who? Me or you?"

"Me."

"You? Marshall got back in this bed so I can push you back out. You sound crazy."

He sat on the floor with his arms wrapped around his bent legs.

"How about what you did hurt me. Just imagine how I felt when I found out the man, no, my husband who I've been trying to have a baby with ends up getting his side chick pregnant before his wife, and then he tried to act like everything is supposed to be all good. Wait, and now I find out its almost instantly after you all met."

"I know Ronnie. That's why I want us to start over. Plus, I think you need to come home and be on a diet. I see you've been eating pretty good wherever you have been staying." He got back in bed.

"Boy stop." I pulled the blanket above my stomach and laid it below my breastbone.

"Is there anything else you would like to know?"

"Yes, I do. How are you going to make this up to me?" I rolled slightly onto my side and rubbed my index finger across his right cheek.

"I don't know you have to tell me what you think I should do. Whatever it is. I got you."

I was so tired of me having to tell him what he should do. Why should I have to tell him what to do and how to do it? After all the time we have been together, he still didn't get it.

"You can start by making me a cup of coffee." I was annoyed with him. I knew I couldn't have coffee because I was pregnant, but if I said a glass of juice, he would've known something was up.

He smiled and walked around the foot of our king size bed and through the doors.

"Make it fast," I yelled, playfully.

I turned on the television and one of my favorite television shows was on. I always thought it should have lasted longer than a half-hour. Marshall wasn't back upstairs yet, and our coffee maker only took 3 minutes to brew up something good. I couldn't get mad because all I would do is flush it down the toilet anyway.

After a while, my feet hit the ground, and I started to walk down the hallway. I couldn't hear anything at first, but I listened to a woman's voice when I got closer to the kitchen. I crept behind the walls leading into the kitchen. Taking a small peek at the back of the Marshalls body. He was standing by the coffee maker that he hadn't even turned on.

"How did your body do after our run this morning?" A shrill voice said on the other end of the phone, which sounded all too familiar minus the high pitch. I started to think the receiver part of his phone was broke. He never cared if I could hear his conversations. He continued to show he just didn't have any respect for me.

Should I run in and a blast his ass?

Should I grab a pan and hit him in the back of his head and knock his ass out?

Instead of doing either of the two, I walked past him unexpectedly without saying a word. Slid my slides on, grabbed the jacket that I haven't worn in ages, and my keys.

Why am I so stupid? I beat on my steering wheel.

I just want someone who loves me.

I put up with this way too long.

When will I give up?

Why haven't I already given up?

My stomach twisted and turned. I opened my car door immediately after pulling into Coles driveway. I barfed all over his driveway pavement, missing the floor of my car. I looked up to see if anyone saw me, instead of being embarrassed, I was shocked. Cole was standing in front of a black vehicle, embracing another woman. One stab in the heart after another. Cole ran toward my car, hysterical.

"I see that you are busy. I'll just come back when you are not busy." I slammed my car door and gripped my gear shift.

"Ronnie, wait," he yelled. "What's wrong?"

"Nothing, I'll just go somewhere to be alone. I see that you and my husband are too busy for me," I yelled out of the window.

"Mr. Williams." The lady walked toward my car. "I forgot to give you this," she extended her arm toward him, handing him a booklet. "I hope I am not interrupting."

"Well, yeah, you are," I screamed at her.

"No... No... You aren't. This is the lady I was telling you about." He looked at me and back at her. "Ronnie, this is nutritionist Harrison. Mrs. Harrison, this is Ronnie." He introduced us.

"Hi, how are you, Ronnie? Make sure your stress level stays down. I don't want you to end up in the ER."

"We will. Thanks for coming out." Cole handed me a paper booklet. "I'll be sure that she follows these instructions."

I opened the brochure. In bold writing, it read, How to stay healthy during pregnancy and ways to keep stress levels down.

"You're welcome," Cole said to me as the nutritionist walked back to her car.

I put my head so far down that my chin touched my chest. My eyes were balled with tears by the time I lifted it back up to look at him.

Cole hurried to open my car door. "Ronnie, she is just a nutritionist. Nothing is going on between us two. I called her for you. I wanted a better insight on how to monitor you, that's all."

"It has nothing to do with you, Cole." I wiped whatever tears I had left in my eyes and another ran down right after. "It's Marshall, he is still being him, and I am still being me. A dumbass."

Cole grabbed my hand and helped me out of the car. "You want me to park it in the garage for you?"

"Sure, that would be great."

The door opened.

"Can you grab our food before you come in?"

He looked at the food in the driver's seat. "What you got me some McQueens? How did you know?" He said with a huge smile.

"Their milkshakes are the bomb, right?" I said over my shoulder, walking to the front door.

Bzzzzzzzzz....

"Wake up sleepyhead," Cole said as he walked over to the alarm to turn it off. "You know this alarm has been going off for like 20 mins."

I stretched and pulled the cover over my head. "But I don't want to get up. Come back later."

Cole laughed. "Do you want me to make you some breakfast?" He had put on a few pounds.

"As always, yes, I do." I stretched every muscle in my body.

"Okay, I'll be back in a minute."

I sat up in bed. My phone laid on the other end of the pillow. It had not been charged since the night before. I waited on my breakfast with nothing to do. So, I checked my Open Chat page. When I signed in, I had fourteen new messages from people I wasn'tn interested in connecting with. I looked through them, and there was no one on there to connect with. There were some people I used to go to school with and didn't care to see. Open Chat app told a lot about people, which made me wonder what type of person Casey was. Why haven't I stalked her page months ago? I scrolled over to her page. She had pictures of her holding her stomach, and some others were selfies and visits to the doctor. Her most recent photo was dated the day before. She was standing on the track that Marshall usually goes running on. It was a full-body picture. So, I had already known that it was Marshall who took it. Tears welled in my eyes and ran down my face after blinking.

Why me?!

Like, what did I do wrong?

Cole walked in with my breakfast. I wiped my eyes before he could see a thing. He laid the plate across my lap.

"Umm...Cole, what the hell is this?"

"It's juice, yogurt, strawberries, eggs, and toast."

"Where is my usual?"

"Hmm... I had to change it up for you. The nutritionist said this would be a healthier breakfast for you."

"Forget the nutritionist, man, I'm hungry. I need some real food Cole before I hop in my car and go to Mc Queens." I moved the food to the side. "You know what don't worry about it. I want to talk to you about something."

"Uh-oh, wait. This doesn't sound good at all."

"No, it shouldn't be bad news for you."

"Well, that's good to hear."

"So, I'll just go ahead and say it. I am thinking about divorcing Marshall," I blurted out.

"Whoa, Ronnie, are you sure about this? This is the father of your child. You can't do something like that to your family," he sounded worried.

"Me? I can't do something like this to my family. Who's side are you on?" I fanned him off and crossed my arms.

"I am on no one's side Ronnie, but you should really think about this." He laid his hand on my leg.

"And I have, and I am going to file for a divorce, as soon as possible."

"But, Ronnie," he said sympathetically.

I stormed out of the room. Did that move look familiar? I yelled, and it echoed through the hallway.

Cole chased me through the hallway. He grabbed me by my shoulder. "Ronnie, talk to me."

"I can't keep going back and forth between you and Marshall. It's not healthy for me, and it's not healthy for the baby. Yesterday Marshall told me he wanted us to start over. I asked him when the last time he saw his baby momma, and he said it had been a while. I walked downstairs to check on the coffee he was supposed to be making me, and he is on the video chatting with her talking about how good their run was they just had before he walked in. He lied to me."

"Okay, but..."

"But what Cole? But what? I think it's best for me to get a divorce. I finally need to choose my path and be at peace. I am going to the courts tomorrow, and I am done talking about it."

I went home to get closure from Marshall and to drop the divorce papers off to him. He pulled out of our driveway and headed down the road. For the hell of it, I followed him. I loved a little adventure, and I wanted to see if he was going to meet up with his baby mama. I stayed one car behind him. I was sure he would spot my car.

He pulled over and parked in front of a grocery store. I parked a couple of cars back across the street. He got out of the car, and he walked into the jewelry store next door. It was the same jewelry store where I picked out my engagement ring. I watched him through the expansive lengthened windows. I always thought about how they should change those windows because you could see directly into the store and see everything that was going on, but that day I was glad they didn't.

As soon as he spoke to one of the employees, I called his phone. Rather than answering like I thought he would, he pulled his phone out, looked at it, and slide it back into his pocket. He paced back and forth from one side of the store to the other for over a half-hour. At the same time, the young blonde Caucasian lady followed on the other side of the counter. He had always been an indecisive person. My stomach sounded like a monster truck was driving in it. I had to eat soon, so to speed up the process. I called the store.

Hello, this is Harrys Jewelers. How can I help you?" The young Caucasian lady said.

Hi, I was looking to buy some jewelry. I can't seem to figure out what to get a certain lover of mine. I was wondering if you could give me a few options.

Well, if you could stop by, that would help because I am actually with a customer right now, and I would like to give you both the best advice.

Oh, okay, is there any chance you can tell me what your client is looking for. Maybe it would be something that I might want to get for myself.

Hmmm. Well, I am working with someone who is looking for an engagement ring.

Click.

I slung my phone onto the passenger side of the car. If I could have ran my car into that jewelry store, I swear I would have. Between being both angry and hungry. I almost turned into incredible hulk. I was going to be easy on him, but it seemed like things had changed. He was trying to marry that bitch.

I called his phone again. He didn't even bother to look at it. So, I texted him.

We need to talk.

I didn't bother to even look at him. I wasn't even expecting a message back.

We sure do.

I get a text back instantly after.

It's funny how...

deleted message

See, this is why...

deleted message

Meet me at Neverland for dinner tonight. I sent the message after deleting the first couple of them.

Sounds like a plan. Marshall replied and put his phone back in his pocket.

I had to stop by McQueens before heading back to Cole's place.

There were many ways I could've presented the divorce papers. I sat in the car and meditated for a bit.

BAM! Slamming the documents on the table. "I want a divorce, Bitch!"

Or maybe I'd sit down first, then BAM. "Sign these papers, Biotch!"

I looked over at the divorce papers that laid in the passenger side seat. I searched everywhere for the red folder I put them in. I put them in a red folder because I was out for blood.

Beep. "Could you please move up?" the person in the car sitting behind me said.

I hadn't realized I was holding up the valet line. I threw my hand up, gesturing an apology. I walked towards the brick building with a Welcome to Neverland sign in the window. I looked around before I walked up to the front desk to check-in. It was packed like sardines, so I searched the room a while before I met with a greeter.

"Can I help?" A tall, slim, long-haired woman said.

"No, I see my company right over there." I spotted Marshall sitting by the waterfall with his hand raised like I was taking attendance. The waterfall in Neverland represented romance and was always a less crowded area.

I had on a tie-dyed sundress with no panties. My panties had gotten too small and tight around my pelvis area. I haven't gone to the store yet to purchase new ones. I placed the folder in front of my belly to hide my baby bump. I walked over to the table, and Thick by O.T Genasis played in my head, and my ass was semi twerking.

"Don't bother," I said to him before he stood up to pull my chair out for me. He had on a light gray slim fit suit with a white-collared shirt.

"So, what did you need to talk to me about?" I laid the folder across my belly.

"Can I get you something to drink?" the waitress said over my shoulder.

I turned toward her. "Can I have a water with lemon?"

"I ordered a bottle of champagne," he said to the waitress.

"Okay, I can bring that out now." She walked off.

"Wow, feels like I haven't seen you in forever."

"You haven't. What's the champagne for?" I tapped my freshly gel full set nails on the table.

"It's a celebration," he smiled with his beautiful teeth, but he wasn't going to have his way. It was a regretful day for him.

"Celebration? A celebration for what?"

"A celebrati—" the waitress walked over and poured us each a glass."

"A celebration for us starting over." He paused and then continued. "Ronnie, I love you, and I just want to make things right. I know I put you through so much, and there is no way I can make it up to you. But because of that, I think we should maybe see other people. That's what I've been thinking for a while now, and I decided.

I looked down and shuffled through the folder before I grabbed it for my solo performance.

"I've decided—"

"You know what I think about your new beginning, huh? I think we should..." BAM! I slapped the folder on the table. "I want a divorce bitch." I looked toward him, and he was longer sitting in his seat. He was on one knee with a ring pointed at me. I was so embarrassed. Not embarrassed that I said I wanted a divorce but embarrassed about thinking he was buying her that ring.

"Oh, Shit," someone said in the background.

I watched everyone put their phones away.

"I decided that I would rather be with you than to be with anyone else." He looked up for the shock of his life. "Ronnie, why didn't you tell me you wanted a divorce before we met here?" he whispered. He got up from the floor slowly. You could tell from his tense shoulders he was a bit of a mess at that point.

"I gave you the same heads up you gave me when you were cheating on me with a girl you went to school with." I didn't want our audience to think I was a cold-hearted bitch so I had to give them the whole story.

"Ronnie, not right now. Not in front of all these people."

"Well, you asked, and I told. Up here trying to make it seem like you are a good guy."

"Ronnie, you know what I meant."

"No, I don't, Marshall."

Marshall threw a couple of dollars on the table. He grabbed me by my arm and directed me to the exit door.

I snatched away. "Don't get fucked up in front of these people," I whispered.

He put his hands in his pocket.

We walked outside, and Marshall paced back in front on the sidewalk. He stomped and jumped across the sidewalk.

The sight was pleasuring. That was the angriest I've ever seen him. It was kind of scary at the same time.

He mumbled to himself, one side of his unbuttoned shirt hung out of the waistline of his pants.

I stood up straight and held my stomach in. I changed my position. I did whenever I had to hide my bulge.

"Ronnie, what made you want this divorce and not tell me? What has gotten into you?" He paced back and forth again.

"Marshall, what made you want to have an affair and not tell me?"

"I'm serious." He walked toward me with fire in his eyes.

The valet driver walked up to us to collect our tickets. Marshall brushed him off, but I gave the valet driver mine.

"Sorry that he is rude. Can you put a rush on my order, though, please?"

"Yes, I am right on it," the short, brown-skinned man said.

Every step Marshall made toward me, I stepped back. I looked behind me every step to make sure I didn't run into anything. I kept stepping back from him until I stumbled against someone's car door.

"I told you I wanted to start over," he retorted.

"Well, it's too late for me," I cut to the right and continued to step back.

The waitress ran out with my red folder. "Sorry to interrupt, but you left the folder inside." She handed me my folder. Her hands were shaky.

Marshall stopped walking toward me. "Don't you understand that I love you?"

I became overwhelmed, nauseated, and dizzy. I hoped

to end this conversation soon before I puked or passed out.

"You know what, Marshall, I don't want to talk about it anymore. Here are the papers." I pushed them into his chest. He lost balance and stepped back.

I walked off, he threw the papers at me, and they flew straight down the sidewalk.

"Now, why the hell did you do that. I'll just have your ass served. I was trying to be nice. The next time you see these papers, go ahead and sign them for I take all yo shit and make it mine. Period," I giggled. Cole would've laughed if he heard me say that word.

Valet pulled up in my car.

"Go get my car," Marshall shouted at the Valet driver.

The driver walked off as if he didn't hear him

"Damn, you are just having a bad day, huh?" I got in my car and put my foot on the ignition and drove off sickly. I waved bye with a smile.

The surge of nausea that hit me was so intense that I hardly made it up the street before I emptied my stomach on the side of the road.

"Are you okay?" A concerned pedestrian asked.

A trail of vomit hung from my bottom lip. I looked up and it was the guy with the expensive cologne, Casey's brother.

"Oh, hey. Are you okay?" he asked walking toward me, but before he could get any closer, I lifted my head back into the car and pulled off.

Bzzz.Bzzz.Bzzz. Lori's name lit in the display.

I wiped my mouth with an old McQueens napkin that I found in my glove compartment.

One hand on the steering wheel and I threw my napkin down with the other. I struggled to get my phone out of my purse. Eventually, I found it buried below.

Yeah, girl. What's going on? I hoped she didn't notice how breathy I sounded.

Nothing, haven't seen you in a while. I wanted to stop by your hotel room. Lori chuckled.

Girl, what's so funny?

Nothing, I am just bothered. You are not staying with me, and I am your whole cousin, but I won't trip.

Well, I just left Marshall right now. I am going to go home and take care of some business. But we can meet at Rosettes tomorrow."

Wait. What? Just left Marshall for what?

Just meet me tomorrow.

"What did you do today?" Cole sat at the end of the bed while gently massaging my feet.

I lifted my back parallel to the backboard. I wrapped my arms around my bent legs. "I thought you would never ask. I met with Marshall today to give him the divorce papers, and at the same time, he was trying to propose to me again."

"Wow, so how did that go?" He continued to massage each toe.

"Well, it didn't go well at all. Marshall got mad and tried to drag me out by my arm."

"He tried to do what," he said furiously. His face shifted as he leaned toward me to get a better listen.

"No, it's okay. I checked him."

"Naw, Imma have to go over there and check him tho."

"No...no...no... sit back down. Everything is okay." I leaned forward and grabbed his arm. "Sit back down. I am fine. I handled it."

"Is he going to sign them?"

"I don't know. I am going to have him served." I laid back on the bed. "Why can't this be simple? Why couldn't he just take the papers and let this be over?"

"Does he know that you are pregnant." He walked around the bed, laid down, and faced me. Cole's eyes had a rare dim in them. He was very sexy but even sexier when upset. "I guess not, because if he did, he would have never touched you how you said he did."

He rolled over, pulled the cover just above his waist. "We can talk more when I wake up."

Cole had been acting strange lately. First, he was angry at me, the next he was happy, and then he started sleeping in the same bed as me.

"Okay, that's fine." I agreed.

I grabbed my phone from my purse that sat on the nightstand. I browsed through different selections of maternity clothes that I had planned on buying once I took Marshall for all he had if he didn't stop playin' with me. Looking through different clothing made me think about Casey. What would she wear? I explored her Open Chat page. One more week and I will know the sex of our baby, her Open Chat page status read.

Doctors office, here I come. I placed my phone back on the nightstand.

I watched some reruns of *Maury* that I recorded on Cole's tv. I loved it when he said, "You are not the father!" then the girls ran off the stage like she didn't know that in the first place.

Bzzzzzzz...

I woke and turned the alarm off. Cole was staring me in the face. "You ready for your first visit?" He smiled as he pressed a kiss on my forehead.

"Awww, you remembered. How sweet of you."

"Yes, what, you think you are the only one on top of this?"

I grabbed his face and kissed him on the lips.

"You want breakfast before you go?"

"Of course, I do." I looked over his shoulder, and he had a big bag of chips and half a bottle of a 2-liter soda. "It looks like you ate already."

"Yeah, but I can eat again."

"Welp let's get to it. I don't want to be late."

"Do you want me to go with you? For comfort?"

"No, I'll be fine. Thanks, though."

I parked in front of my doctor's office, hoping that the gynecologist didn't remember the fart I set off in her office the last time I was there. I stared at the tall 40 story building. I wanted to pull off, but something said stay and get a check-up. That was supposed to be a happy moment for me, but it was more confusing. Marshall should've been with me. That was our baby. But instead I was alone and was sharing him with someone else.

My shorts didn't zip up anymore. So, I wrapped a shirt around my waist and tied a knot in it. My small baby bump still protruded over my zipper. Instead of stalking Casey page, I should've ordered me some new clothes like I started to.

I walked over to the elevator. My head was spinning, and I began to feel like I was on a big ship being rocked back and forth by waves. After a while, I couldn't take it anymore. I ran toward the nearest bathroom, but before I made it one step past the door, I puked on the all-white marble floors right next to the door leading into the men's bathroom.

I was nowhere near embarrassed about puking in public because I had other things going on in my life that were much more embarrassing than a little vomit .

"Are you okay?" overlapping voice shouted in my background. Several people were trying to assist me.

"I'm fine," I replied.

"I'll help you to sit down.' A woman volunteered.

When I sat down, I realized how serious being pregnant was going to be for me. Did I want to divorce Marshall and raise a baby all alone? Being pregnant took a lot of time and dedication, and I wasn't even halfway through my pregnancy yet.

I sat at a black steel table at Rosettes waiting for Lori. The waitress walked over, placed some ice water on the table, and handed me a more cushioned chair. I knew if he knew I was pregnant, Lori would surely figure it out once she saw me.

"Thank you." He helped push me up to the table.

Lori walked through the door. She has a bouquet of roses and a bottle of champagne in her hand. I knew she would find out after I told her I couldn't pour up with her.

I raised from my chair and strolled toward her. I placed my shawl around my arms and wrapped it across and over my opposite shoulder.

She walked toward me with her arms extended, ready for the biggest hug. She approached me and looked me up and down like she didn't know who I was. Her face looked like she just sucked on a lemon. Real sour-ish. I hoped I didn't smell pregnant, whatever that smelled like.

Once, she got a full look at me. She hugged me and squeezed me like she was trying to squeeze the last drop out of a ketchup bottle.

I kinda brushed her off me slowly because of the pain

and pressure on my stomach.

"So how many months are you?" She stood back and laid her hand on my stomach.

Did she talk to cole?

The waiter?

How the hell did she know I was pregnant?

"What do you mean, how many months?

"Bitch, don't play with me. You have on a shawl. I've never seen that shawl a day in my life, and its fucking 80 degrees outside, and your stomach punched me in my damn stomach. So, I'll ask again, how many months are you?" She cocked her head and placed her hand on her hip.

"I knew I couldn't hide anything from you. I don't know why I try." I shook my head.

"I don't know either, but answer the question."

"Damn, I am two months and some change."

"What do you mean, some change?" she pressured me.

"Around two months and a week."

"So am I invited to the ultrasound."

"I'll have to let you know."

"Girrrlll, don't play with me." She gave me a blank stare. Her face looked like it was about to fall off. "But, anyway, O-M-G!" She jumped up and down, yelled, spun, and ran in a circle. "OMG! I can't believe this. So, when were you going to tell me?" she frowned and took a step back.

"Girl, are you bipolar? Can you slow down? Can we just sit down?"

"So, when were you going to tell me?" she repeated as she pulled out my chair to sit.

"Helping me sit down. I could get used to this," I joked. I took my shawl off and threw it across the seat next to me.

"I was going to tell you right now." I lied.

"Well, I am so happy for you?" She congratulated me. "What did Marshall say?

"Marshall doesn't know yet, and I plan on keeping it that way. So, don't you say a word to anyone? Not even to my mom."

"Damn, so you just low key, huh?"

"Yes, I had him served. We are getting a divorce."

"Ronnie?"

"Lori?"

"Ronnie, you are pregnant. Why would you want to get a divorce?"

"Well, he does have another baby on the way, so he will not miss me too much."

"You are his wife."

"She is his side chick. Maybe even his roommate once he signs those papers. He just better not give me any trouble or I'll take all his shit. Plus, I am moving to New York. I have a job offer, and then I can work on my firm out there."

"Wait. First, you are pregnant, then you are getting a divorce, and now you are moving. This news is a lot to lay on your best friend/cousin at one time. This shit hurt Ron." She grabbed a napkin from the table and wiped the tears fallen from her face. "This shit hurts Ron. You are honestly going to leave me. You and my god baby," she sobbed.

"How in the hell are you going to just name yourself the god mommy?"

"Bitch, you ain't got no damn friends, Tf?!" she continued to wipe the tears from your eyes. "Have you discussed this with anyone else? Does anyone know about this dumb ass decision you are making?" She tried to make light of the situation. Laughing to keep me from crying, and that's what she and I do best.

"No, I haven't." I lied.

"I need you to get it together, Ronnie? You have to at least tell your mom about what's going on."

"No, I don't, and you don't either?"

"So, when did you find out about all of this?

"I found out that night you went over to scare Marshall. You scared me so bad that I ended up in the hospital."

"Oh no, I am sorry. That's not a good way to find out that you were pregnant. You went by yourself?" She picked up her menu and stuffed her face in the middle of it.

I think Lori was catching on to what I've been doing. She knows me too well. She always knew when I was lying.

"Yes, I went by myself." I lied. "I know I should've called you." I gave a fake smile.

"Ron, it's something that you are not telling me."

"Girl, why do you always think someone is keeping something from you."

"Not someone...you...I know you too well."

I waved the waitress down so he could come over and take our order. I was too hungry. "Everything is going to be okay, Lori. Now, what do you want to eat." I reached for my water. The ice cubes had already evaporated.

I couldn't believe that it was about to go down. I pulled into the parking lot of the courthouse. All those years putting up with Marshall shit was about to come to an end. I couldn't wait to till it was all over with to tell him I was finally pregnant. He wouldn't be too worried about me, but it would hurt him to have to take care of two babies. I knew he would be with her, and I didn't want my baby around that bitch. Better yet, I wouldn't tell him and if he ever asked in the future. I planned on telling him it was someone else's, and it happened after the divorce.

My belly grew bigger and bigger, and I stayed trying to find ways to cover it up. It wasn't too hard though, since my stomach hadn't really turned into a full baby bump yet. I wore a bright yellow sundress with my fanny pack strapped loosely around my belly. When you had all that ass I had you had to have some type stomach anyway. He wouldn't had notice like Lori because I hadn't planned to hug his ass.

I carried the letter with the information on it. I walked off the elevator down the long hall to the office. Room 2130b was down the hall and to the left around the first corner. I made sure to look at the directory. I had no time to get lost. I needed tp end our marriage as quickly as possible. The end was near as I got closer and closer to the room.

"Hello?" I said to the janitor. She was a little older than me. She was holding her back while sweeping.

"Hello?" she spoke back.

"Room 2130b is this way, right?" I pointed straight down the hall.

I spoke to everyone I walked past that day. I never knew who I would need to have my back while I was there. I hoped I'd run into his lawyer and sweet talk him into telling Marshall to sign the papers and get everything over with stat.

My palms sweated profusely. I stood before the door

for about a minute before I knocked.

"Come in," A loud voice yelled from the other side.

I opened the door slowly and it swung to my right. The view of the freshly cleaned window cleared my mind. You got this bitch. I walked in the peppermint-scented room and looked to my left, where everyone sat. Marshall and his lawyer sat across from my lawyer and an empty chair waiting for me to sit and join the conversation.

I pranced over to my seat that my lawyer had gotten up and pulled out for me. The scent of peppermint became more and more overwhelming and made me queasy.

"Hi, how are you, Mrs. Valentine?" Marshall's lawyer greeted me.

"It's Miss Lawson." I corrected him.

"It's not Miss Lawson until we sign the papers and get this settled," Marshall inserted. He had a big attitude.

"Okay, let's just get started," My lawyer said, saving the day. "We are here because my client would like a divorce. She said you could have everything but the house. If you agree, please sign by the x, and we can move forward," my lawyer instructed. She pulled a sheet from the bundle of papers sitting in front of her.

"My client would like to know the reason why Miss. Lawson wants a divorce in the first place."

I whispered in my lawyer's ear.

"My client said she would not like to answer that question seeing how he already knows. She would just like to get this over with so they both can move on."

"I know your little secret," Marshall said, with pleasure.

My body stiffened. I tried to extend my right arm

to grab the napkin box, and it wouldn't move. I tried to speak, but my mouth dropped and stayed. My chest tightened. My stomach twist and turned. I couldn't hold it anymore.

He knew. He knew. Who could've told him?

My stomach felt weak, and vomit erupted in me like a volcano. Everyone jumped back from their seats. There was vomit splattered all over the table.

"Are you okay?" Everyone said in unison.

I reached to grab some napkins. Marshall snatched some and placed them in my hand.

"Ronnie, are you okay?" He looked uneasy.

"Yes, I am okay. Damn. I had sushi for dinner last night." I lied. I wiped all the residue that I could from my month.

"But you don't like sushi." He reminded himself.

"I know. That's probably why I am throwing it up." I continued to lie. "Now, let's get back to business."

Everyone sat back in their seats.

Marshall fixed his suit before he slid his chair back under the table.

My lawyers tried to recover all the papers that she could.

"Okay, if you can just sign here, we can all go," I suggested. I was lucky my lawyer was able to recover the main page from the bundle.

"Now, I know your little secret. Would you like to explain to me why you want to move to New York?"

My body loosened. I took a deep breath. I was relieved. "How do you know that I am moving to New York?"

"Well, your mom called me, and she said that Lori told her."

"Is that all Lori told her, or is there something else that I need to know?" I questioned bug-eyed.

"That's all your mom told me. Is there something else that I should know?"

"Is there something else I should know?" I counter challenged.

"Yes, you should know if you go to New York. I want part of your firm."

"Well, you should know, you are not getting part of shit and I am on their ass for telling you my business. You and I are not cool, and you don't need to know anything about me outside of signing these papers."

"Ronnie, you can't leave."

"Oh, so you want me to stay here while you raise your bastard child. I think not."

The janitor walked in to clean up my vomit.

"I am sorry. I lost control of myself. I don't think that the sushi I ate last night agreed with me." I apologized about a lie.

"It's okay, ma'am," she replied.

"Let me know if there is anything, I could do for you. You are supposed to be picking up papers and not nasty things like this." I gave her one of my cards. "This card is the only thing I have with my number."

"Okay, thank you so much. Suppose I need someone to talk to, I'll call you." The janitor exited the room.

"Now, back to you." I held up my index finger and shook it at him for a warning. I leaned over the table with my index finger extended towards his face. "You are not getting any part of my firm. Never will you ever get anything I've worked hard for. Now sign the damn papers before I sign off on some alimony checks."

I am a divorced woman!

CHAPTER 10

Miss. Lawson

I laid in my bed and stared out through my bedroom windows, perplexed, and confused. I tried to figure out why in the hell did my ex-husband think he deserved half ownership of my new firm? When he didn't do a damn thing but give me gray hairs while trying to get started. The beautiful orange and red tones that beamed through my floor to ceiling windows made me feel grateful to be alive—what a lovely ass day.

I gazed around at what I had accomplished. My eyes stopped to admire my high vaulted ceiling's views in my big ass, beautiful home. I dreamt about having a house like that, and I worked so hard to get it. Now that I had it all to myself made it much more rewarding. *Boom.* I turned toward the television. My favorite movie came on. Perfect timing.

My scorching hot coffee burned the tip of my tongue and left it numb, but that didn't stop me from continuing to drink and pleasure myself with my favorite vanilla flavor coffee, two creams, and two sugars. My silk sheets felt so good against my freshly waxed and washed skin. My shower the night before mixed with my exfoliating cream made me feel like a brand-new woman. The central air kicked on, and I pulled my covers up past my waist. I knew it was going to be a great day.

My phone had been buzzing and flashing for about 30 minutes. I decided to see who had been calling. I reached over to grab the thing that caused so many problems. I had twenty-three missed calls and fifteen text messages. It was nobody but my ex-husband of course. For the life of me I couldn't figure out why he had been so upset.

The phone rang in the palm of my hand. What the hell did he want? In a low and raspy tone. "Hello, who is this... I mean, who do I have the pleasure of speaking with?" I snickered.

"Why have you been ignoring my calls?" he yelled.

"Look, Marshall. I don't have time for the small talk right now or ever again. There is nothing for us to say to one another. Which one of us had an affair, huh?"

"What the hell are you talking about? Ronnie, we need to talk!"

I hung up. Ha. Ha. Ha. Ha. If Marshall thought he could check me, he had another thang coming.

"Hellooooo, what the hell so funny? Why are you laughing?" A voice came from the receiver's end of the phone.

"Oh shit." I clicked the end button. I tossed myself on my bed. Wow, now that was funny as hell.

Boom. Boom. Boom. Thrilling sounds made me turn cheerfully towards the television. It was the part in the movie when Carmen bangs on the door of her ex-lover. She showed up to his place unannounced finds out he had a wife. Well, Carmen should've never cheated. Maybe she would still have her man. I guess that's the same anger Marshall had, but he had to know that what goes around comes around. It's called karma, bitch.

I started another movie. My body felt like a loaf of potatoes. My eyes shifted over at my nightstand, the eight by ten picture collage of Marshall and me when we met back in college, when I graduated from law school, and the day we got married was still standing up. I reached over, grabbed the picture, and placed it face down. I threw it away soon after.

"What the hell are you doing here?" A knock on the window followed.

I looked up from my phone; my heart pounded from being startled.

"Are you following me?" Casey asked, sounding flustered.

I had been following her. She took so damn long to get out of the car that I started to look at some new shoes. The ones I had on were not giving me any more support.

I eyed her standing on the side of my driver's side door before I rolled down my window. She looked like she gained about 20 lbs, if not more. She wore a white spaghetti string top that fitted tightly around her watermelon shaped stomach. "Why would you think someone is following you?" I crossed my arms.

She placed her hand on her hip then rubbed her stomach. Her freshly done full set nails reminded me of cat woman. "Ronnie, I knew this was your car, and you had been following me for a while."

"Girl wasn't nobody following you." I lied. "Now, go back to your car and mind your business."

"Girl, stop playing with me. I was just talking to Marshall about it, and he told me your driver's license plate number. So, I knew it was you for about two miles." She tried to bend over as much as her stomach would allow so her eyes could level with mine for a stare-off.

I turned my head to break eye contact and focused them on the Advocate Medical Center sign across the parking lot. "Okay, that doesn't mean I was following you. I have some business up here too at advocate." I lied, again. I looked back at her, hoping she was looking the other way and not focused on my answers' vagueness or my rapid blinking.

"Why have you been in your car as long as I've been in mine? I know you are following me. You could've taken a different and shorter way to this same hospital, but you ended up right behind me."

"Please step away from my vehicle Casey. I don't have time for this. I have things to do."

I uncrossed my arms without thinking of its impact.

She looked at me, then my arms, and then finally my stomach that sat on top of my steering wheel's bottom. "Is there something you want to tell me?" she stood up straight. Her upper body leaned further back than her bottom, losing her balance. The hair on her lace front wig needed to be glued on much better and blew in the wind.

"No," I crossed my arms back across my stomach.

"I'll leave, for now, Ronnie. But you just wait, and oh yeah, I know about your little divorce, but did you know about our engagement. She flashed her hand, and her ring finger sparkled.

"I am not bothered by that little ring sweetheart, because that ring is a pass down from me. Check with your husband, he will tell you about it, ' i laughed.

"Trick whatever. Have a great day because I sure will. I am about to have the life you've always wanted."

Both of my fists clenched. But I thought about the failures that Marshall and I had and brushed it off. "That's okay. I wouldn't want to live your life. Hence the divorce," I snickered.

"Girl bye." She wobbled off.

I wasn't going to waste my time going after her. I could barely move. After seeing that ring, I promised that time would be the last time I ever planned to stalk her.

As she walked through the parking lot to the hospital's entryway, the path to exit the parking lot crossed paths with her. I rode past her, flipped her the bird while blasting "Bitches ain't Shit" by Dr. Dre singing loud and in sync with the song.

"Why are you sitting out here?"

I looked up and saw Cole stood over me. I didn't hear him come out of the house. I was so into my thoughts about Marshall proposing to Casey with the ring he used to propose to me. I didn't know if I should feel any way at all, knowing that I divorced him.

"Why are you sitting out here?" Cole repeated before he sat on the side on me on his brick patio. He wore a white tank top and tan cargo shorts.

"Just thinking?" I looked down at the concrete ground.

"Yes, I see that. You have been out here for a minute. I decided to come to check on you." Cole put his hand on my thigh, rocked it back and forth, and then placed both his hands in his pocket. "What's wrong? You want to talk about it?"

"Naw, I'd rather keep this embarrassment to myself." I placed my hair behind my ear with my long thin finger.

"C'mon Ronnie. You have to tell me what's wrong. It's never good to keep stress held inside. It's not good for the baby. Let it out." He bat his eyelashes at me and smiled.

"I see you have a haircut." I stared him in his eyes and

rubbed his hair in the direction he always brushed it.

He grabbed my hand and placed it on the concrete space that separated us. "Ronnie, I wanna know what's wrong, but if you don't want to talk about it. Me and my new haircut will go back into the house."

Cole's eyes sparked, and he looked very handsome. Those eyes made me tell him everything. "Okay, here it is. Marshall proposed to Casey with the ring he proposed to me with."

Cole leaned to the side with a smirk on his face. "Ronnie, that seems like a blessing to me. I don't know why it would be so bad. Now it's her problem to deal with."

"I put a lot of pain and suffering into that relationship and look at what happened; he goes and gets a bitch pregnant. What a jab in my face."

"Well, you have a sweet baby coming. That will be your best friend forever, and they'll never hurt you. Think about your future, Ronnie. You are smart and beautiful. Believe me when I tell you that your life is going to be fair for you from now on." He leaned over and placed a kiss on my forehead.

"Thanks, Cole. That was sweet."

"If you ever need anything, I am here for you." He stood up and took my hand to stand up with him. "Now let us go into the house. So, I can cook you up a meal."

Hello, this is Early Detect Center. This is James speaking. How can I help you?

Hello, I was calling to schedule an appointment.

Okay, can I have your name?

Ronnie. Ronnie Lawson.

Ronnie Lawson, I see the last person you talked to here was Cathy. Would you like to schedule with her?

Yes, that would be fine.

We have an open appointment tomorrow at noon. Is that okay?

Yes, sure, that's fine.

Okay, we will see you tomorrow.

"What did they say?" Cole said, sitting in front of me, chewing a piece of filet migeon.

"I have an appointment tomorrow at noon." I gulped down whatever orange juice I had left.

"You want me to go with you for moral support?" He reached over and placed his hand on top of mine.

"No, I think you coming with me would be so wrong in so many ways."

"Maybe I could sit in the car," he insisted.

I moved my hand from under his, propped my elbow on the countertop, and put my cheek into the palm of my hand.

"I could maybe sit in the car," he repeated differently, the same idea.

"I'll be fine. Maybe I'll let you mail it off for me."

Early Detect Center. How can I help you?

Yes, I was calling because I sent in a DNA test. Well, let rephrase that. My friend sent in my DNA test, and I haven't received any results.

I would love to help you. When did you send it off?

They were supposed to have sent send the results off about three days ago.

What's your name?

My name is Ronnie Lawson.

Oh, hey, Ronnie. This is Cathy.

I knew you sounded familiar. I laughed.

No, Ronnie, we don't have your results in the system. I also don't see anything saying we even got anything from you. Would you like me to have them send you another one?

Yes, please. That would be great. You know what, let me check with my friend first, and I'll call back.

Okay, but since it's been a couple of days, it would be best to take another one. So, the results can be more accurate.

Okay, then that would be fine. Thanks a lot, Cathy.

You're welcome.

Bye.

Click

I placed my phone in the cupholder.

"Welcome to Mc. Queens. Can I take your order?" A soft sounded woman said on the intercom.

"Yes. Can I have three chocolate milkshakes, two cheeseburgers, and three fries? Thanks."

I reached to grab my phone and texted Cole. I had to see what why there was a mix-up.

Hey, I called the center to see if they got my results from the DNA test, and they said they didn't get it. You sent it off, right?

Three dots popped up for about two minute in the text screen before getting a reply.

Yes, I mailed it the other day.

I drove up some to keep my place in line at the drive through. *Well, I had them send out another one. We have to do it again, and I'll send it off this time.*

Ok. That's cool, but I don't know why the center hasn't gotten them yet.

I threw my phone into the passenger seat and grabbed my large order from the heavy-set lady standing at the window. She was regular at the window, and I was a regular customer.

"Thank you, love!"

"Thanks for coming to Mc. Queens, again," we both laughed.

Gale was watering her grass when I pulled up in front of my house. Marshall had no longer stayed with me. He packed all his shit up and left. Just how I wanted it. But for some reason, I didn't know why every time I stepped into my house, I felt some guilt.

"Ronnie," Gale yelled from across our attached yards, standing on her tipping toes. I guess she thought her voice would be louder an inch off the ground. She wore a green nightgown, ankle socks, and house shoes.

"Hey Gale, what's going on?"

"Marshall just left here." She walked over to my side of the yard. She pointed at my stomach. "OMG! I didn't know. Congratulations. When's the baby shower?"

I wore a ribbed midi dress with rhinestone-studded slides. I still hadn't bought me any comfortable shoes or clothes.

"I'm not sure yet, Gale, but let's keep this a secret."

"Well, it's going to be hard keeping this a secret. If anybody looks at you, they will know.

"I know, Gale. Seem like I blew up overnight."

"You did. I saw you the other day, and you were barely showing." She reached over to touch my stomach.

"Yeah, Gale, but let's keep between us, okay?" I let her touch my stomach in hopes she wouldn't say anything to Marshall in return.

"You know I got your back, Ronnie."

"Thanks, Gale, and I'll give Marshall a call."

"That's probably why he stopped by, huh? To check on his baby?"

"I doubt it, Gale."

"You need some help with getting your food inside?"

"I could use your help," we laughed

Gale wasn't so bad, after all.

Before I walked in, I grabbed the mail. There was a piece of mail addressed to Marshall.

"Marshall looked in there before he left, but the mailman delivered the mail about a half an hour after he pulled off," Gale informed.

We walked in over to the island, and I placed my phone, purse, and the food that I carried inside the house down. Gale sat the food she carried down on the table.

"I am going to go to the bathroom. You can stay for a while if you want."

"No, I would love to, but I have to head back out and finish doing some gardening." She hit the palm of her hand on her forehead. "I almost forgot."

"I'm sorry I never called you back. I've been so busy. Was it important?"

"Well, not anymore, it seems like you guys are happy now."

"Why would you say that?"

"It's just that Marshall had a young lady around here pretty often when you were gone, but it doesn't matter now...but let me go ahead and get back to my yard."

"Okay, the--"

"Do not forget to send me an invite." She reminded me.

"I won't. Thanks for helping."

"You're welcome. Bye."

I sat on the toilet and debated on opening Marshall's mail, but hell, it came to my house. He needed to get a change of address and fast if he didn't want me in is business. So yeah, I opened it, and he wouldn't find out anyway.

Fertility Clinic was printed in small legible writing in the left top part of the envelope. I slide my finger between the crease of the envelope to opened it.

Dear Marshall Valentine,
The doctor would like for you to come into the clinic to discuss your result. Please call us at your earliest convenience to set up an appointment.
Thanks,
Ph.D. Williams.

I rushed to my purse. I fumbled through it, digging through the other mail I had placed in there. I texted Marshall.

Aye, I have some mail for you here. We can meet up, and I could give it to you.

Can I meet you at the house instead? I need to talk to you about something.

No, that wouldn't be a good idea. We can meet at Rosettes.

"Lawson, reservation for two," the newly employed waitress yelled.

I waved to the waitress, reassuring her it was my reservation.

"Okay, right this way." I followed her over to seats that faced the front door.

"Can I have a cushion, please? Mike knows what I am talking about."

"Yes, I'll be sure to ask." The greeter walked away.

I sat looking out of the window toward the door. Marshall's mail stuck halfway out of my purse. It became jam-packed in line, and I was happy because even with a reservation I would've had to wait in line.

My phone buzzed in my purse. Marshall's name lit up in the display.

I am waiting outside in the long line. I'll be in shortly. Are you here yet?

Yes, I am here. I'll have someone come out and get you.

Okay.

I laid my phone on the shiny wooden table that was big enough for a party five.

Mike walked up shortly with my cushion.

"Thanks, Mike." He turned to walk away. "Mike, can you do me a favor?" He turned back to face me. "My plus one is waiting outside in line. Could you go out to get him for me, Pl-leaze?"

"Sure, what's his name?"

"His name is Marshall.

"Oh, your husband?"

"Ex-husband...Ex-husband."

"Oh, and congratulations on your bundle of joy."

"Thanks, Mike."

Damn, I forgot that fast. Marshall would see it too. I wanted to leave immediately, but I also wanted to know what the mail was all about.

Marshall stepped inside the door, and I waved for him to walk my way.

He wore a red fitted cap, a wrinkled white v neck shirt, and a pair of red cargo shorts.

As he got closer, his eyes were red, and underneath his eyes hung dark and bulky bags.

He pulled his seat out, and before he sat down, he took the shoulder sleeve from his shirt, placed it over his face, and wiped it cleaned.

He gathered himself together and finally sat down.

"I fucked up, Ronnie. I..I...I really fucked up."

"Huh, what are you talking about, Marshall?"

"I mean. I fucked up everything. Everything between us." He reached across the table and tried to grab my hands.

"Everything happens for a reason." I pulled my hands back from him.

"Before I say what I have to say. What is it you wanted to talk about? You asked me to meet you here."

"Well, you got some mail from a fertility clinic."

He put his head down and wept.

"Marshall, why are you crying?"

"I fucked up, Ronnie. I proposed to a bitch. A bitch that's not even going to have my baby."

A small grin came across my face but disappeared as fast as it came.

"The bitch...this bitch." He banged his fist on the table and everyone turned to look at us. "She lied, Ronnie...She lied," he continued, with his rant.

"What did she lie about? Marshall tell me."

"She isn't pregnant with my baby. I am engaged to a motherfucking manipulator."

"Well, that's a good thing that she isn't pregnant by you. Now you can move on or stay with her. I don't know."

"But Ronnie, I fucked it up between us, and now this bitch lied to me. All I wanted was a baby."

I tried to scout my chair further under the table so he wouldn't see my belly.

"How do you know she lied?"

"Ronnie, I can't have kids." He placed his head on the

table again.

"How do you know, Marshall? What do you mean you can't have kids, Marshall?"

"Got dammit. I can't have kids. What does the letter in your purse say?"

I pulled the letter from my purse and slid it to him.

"You opened it?"

"Yeah, by mistake. I thought it had something to do with us." I lied, and I turned to look out of the window and then back at Marshall.

"I called them Ronnie. I am sterile. I can't have kids."

"Wait; what?"

OMG! My baby couldn't possibly be his.

"Are you sure?"

He looked up from the letter. "Yes, and you don't have to hide it, Ronnie. I know that you are pregnant. Casey told me she saw you in the Early Detect Center. I guess that's why she was there too, huh? Picking up a test for herself. But, how? When? Where was I? Your baby is not mine either. I am so hurt."

It's called karma bitch.

"But, Marshall, how could this happen?"

"Remember back in college. I was taking those steroids. You know the rest," he cried.

"I'm so sorry, Marshall." I walked over to his side of the table and sat next to him. I grabbed him by his head and laid it on my shoulder. The same thing I did in college when he found out he couldn't play in his football games anymore.

"Everything will be okay. Just give it time."

He looked up at me and shook his head from side to side and stared out the window opposite from where I sat.

"Is there anything that you can do?"

"They say—" he started.

My phone rang.

"Excuse me."

I walked back around the table where my purse sat in my chair. I pulled it from the side pocket.

Cathy Early Detect Center name lit up in the display.

I turned and looked a Marshall. "I could call them back, if.."

"No, I'll be fine. Go ahead and take it."

"I mean, if right now isn't a good time. I could go ahead and give them a call back later."

"Ronnie, just take the call. I'll be fine."

"It'll just be quick."

Marshall placed his head into his crossed arm that sat on the wooden table.

I quickly pressed the answer button before the call disappeared.

Hello?

Yes, may I speak with Ronnie Lawson?

Hi, this is she.

Hey, this is Cathy.

Oh, hey, Cathy.

Marshall looked up at me with a rise in his slashing eyebrow.

Hey, we got your results. When I talked to you, the system wasn't updated yet, but I could go ahead and send the results over to the email you provided.

I turned with my back facing Marshall. Something I should've done before answering in the first place. Okay, that'll be fine.

I am sending it right over. Have a great day.

Thank you so much, Cathy. You do the same.

I placed my phone back into the side pocket of my purse and placed my purse on the table.

I looked up at Marshall as I sat back down. "I'm sorry about that. Now, where were we?"

"Woooooow, Casey was telling the truth."

"Huh?"

"What you mean, huh?

"Like, the bitch told the truth about what exactly?"

"See, I did not want to believe her." He wiggled his index finger back and forth at me.

"Believe her about what Marshall?"

"If it's not one thing, it's another. Both of you guys truly were playing me."

"Now Marshall, don't go there now. I don't want to get upset right now."

"I am the one that's upset. All this time, I thought you were this sweet innocent little wife."

"Whatever Marshall. Now tell me what your little bitch was right about."

"I can't believe this."

"You know what Marshall...How about I just leave. I wish you nothing but the best." I grabbed my purse from the table and struggled to stand up.

"Nah... Nah... Nah. I'll tell you, but I need you to sit right there and face me so I can see your face once I drop this bomb on you."

I turned back around to face him.

"You know what, let's get a drink." He suggested.

"Yeh, lets." I agreed.

I tracked down the waitress. Before she could approach the table, he yelled, ignorantly. "Can I have a vodka straight up, and she'll have." He looked over at my stomach. "She'll have a cranberry, I guess," he said snappily.

"Okay, Marshall. Now tell me."

"Well, you know the name, Casey Cox."

"Duh!"

"You know the name, Cathy Cox."

I just knew he wasn't going to say what I thought he was...

"Well, they are mom and daughter."

...about to say.

"Remember, I said she saw you pickin' up a test? Well she said you picked up a test from her mother. You had an appointment with her mother, Ronnie."

I stared out of the window. I didn't put two and two together. I mean, Casey and her mom weren't the only people who's last name was cox. I mean, I went to school with a guy who last name cox.

"Oh really.... So did she tell you this before or after she was picking up her test?"

"You know what, Ronnie, you could never make the conversation peaceful. I don't know why I trusted you in the first place. You were nothing but a whore."

"Marshall, don't try to upset me because your ass got played. Don't take me there. Things could get ugly."

"You were playing me the whole time. I knew you weren't shit."

"Marshall, let me tell you about yourself. That little story about you not feeling like a man because you didn't have money. You could never be a man with or without the money. Men have sperm and that's something you lack."

He cocked his head sideways.

"Me paying the bills was me taking care of me. You were just there. I knew about your little girls you always had on the side, but I also knew that karma would catch up with yo ass."

"Ronnie, at the end of the day you aint shit."

"I might not be shit, but I do have a baby that's in me and guess what. It's not yours." I smirked. "Now, my aint shit ass and my baby will be leaving." I flipped him the bird. It took a minute for me to gather my things and headed toward the door, but eventually I left.

We sat in front of my computer and waited for the results. I already knew what they were but I still hoped for a different outcome. Cole sat right beside me with his left hand rubbing my back for comfort. "Sign in already," he said anxiously.

I look at him in his gray eyes, waiting for the courage. "Okay, I have to remember my login." I knew my login. I was stalling.

"Can you go get me something to drink? I am a little parched," I coughed.

"Girl, if you don't open up this email before the password expires." He looked back at the computer keyboard waiting for me to start typing in my username.

"Why are you so anxious? You strapped up, remember?"

"Yeah, but I was hoping I could be the babies godfather." He joked. "But no, I just want to be sure, you know. I've had my doubts, but I just want to be certain."

"Yeah, I understand."

I positioned my fingers on the keyboard and typed away. A link titled Ronnie Lawson results stared back at us. "Can you please go get me something to drink?" I repeated.

"Yes, I'll go get you something right after you click that link." He pointed at the link. His index finger touched the screen. "Dang girl, hurry up," he shouted.

I hovered the mouse over the link, and before I knew it, Cole hit the enter button and the results were sitting right in front of our eyes.

Cole, you are the father.

After Cole jumped for joy and pulled newly bought baby clothes from his walk-in closet, he came over, pulled me up by my wrist for me to stand. He looked me in my eyes and said: "I love you and thank you for this blessing."

Before I knew it, I said, "I love you too, and you're welcome."

He grabbed me by my cheeks with the palms of his hands, pulled me closer to him and laid a powerful kiss on my lips. "I am going to give ya'll the world." He rubbed my stomach, grabbed his phone, and ran to his on-suite bathroom.

"Dad...Dad... I'm going to be a dad, too," he shouted, and his joy was very visible when he jumped up and down.

At that very moment, I was as happy as I've ever been my whole life.

Cole was so anxious to have a half birthday party for Cole Jr. Cole Jr. was only six months and his dad bought out the movie theatre and invited our family and friends and of course Cole Jr. baby friends to see the new kids' movie that the critics raved about.

Lori was now two months pregnant and engaged to a guy she had been seeing for a whole year before I met him. He asked me if he could propose to her at my baby shower and I politely said yes.

"This is so nice. It's like a hundred people here." Lori complimented Cole Jr.'s party. "I can't wait to have my baby. I hope it's a boy so they can be best friends like us." She wrapped her right arm around me and squeezed me to her side. "So how is the firm going. It's been three months already. Wow." She unwrapped me.

"It's going great. I just hired three new people." I fixed my shirt that she wrinkled from our hug.

"Hey, Miss Lawson. Thanks for the invite."

"Girl, no problem. Hope you are having a nice time."

"Yes, I sure am."

"Thanks again and see you back at the office." She walked off.

"Who was that?" Lori asked.

"She is my new secretary. She was the janitor in the office building where I got my divorce."

"A janitor turned secretary. You always did have a kind heart. With yo mean ass," we laughed.

"But I know your commute to work is a breeze."

"Girl, yes. Less than 30 minutes away."

"I am so happy for you, Ron." She smiled.

"Ronnie, do you have anything you want to add," Cole said from a distance.

That was my cue. He held Cole Junior up on his hip. You could never get him to put Junior down. I stood up and gathered my clothes. "Thank you, everyone, for coming out and enjoying Junior's birthday with us. We really can't thank you enough for the support. Hope to see you in six months. Ha.ha.ha."

I sat down and admired Cole from a distance. He has been the best thing that happened to Junior and I. Him and I moved from our old neighborhood and stay about seven houses away from each other now. We decided to just co-parent, and so far, everything has been great. I decided that I needed some me time.

I am now a businesswoman, a valued woman, and a divorced woman. It is now time for me to have my happily ever after.

The End.